TALES OF
EAST AFRICA

TALES OF
EAST AFRICA

FOLKTALES FROM
Kenya, Uganda, and Tanzania

ILLUSTRATIONS BY
Jamilla Okubo

CHRONICLE BOOKS
SAN FRANCISCO

Library of Congress Cataloging-in-Publication Data available.

ISBN 978-1-4521-8258-2

Manufactured in China.

Design by Maggie Edelman.

Illustrations by Jamilla Okubo.

10 9 8 7 6 5 4 3

Chronicle books and gifts are available at special quantity discounts to corporations, professional associations, literacy programs, and other organizations. For details and discount information, please contact our premiums department at corporatesales@chroniclebooks.com or at 1-800-759-0190.

Chronicle Books LLC
680 Second Street
San Francisco, California 94107
www.chroniclebooks.com

"If this story is good, the goodness belongs to all; if it is bad,
the badness belongs only to him who told it."

——GEORGE W. BATEMAN,

"Haamdaanee"

CONTENTS

TRICKSTERS

THE HARE and the LION

Tanzania

One day Soongoo'ra, the hare, roaming through the forest in search of food, glanced up through the boughs of a very large calabash tree, and saw that a great hole in the upper part of the trunk was inhabited by bees; thereupon he returned to town in search of some one to go with him and help to get the honey.

As he was passing the house of Boo'koo, the big rat, that worthy gentleman invited him in. So he went in, sat down, and remarked: "My father has died, and has left me a hive of honey. I would like you to come and help me to eat it."

Of course Bookoo jumped at the offer, and he and the hare started off immediately.

When they arrived at the great calabash tree, Soongoora pointed out the bees' nest and said, "Go on; climb up." So, taking some straw with them, they climbed up to the nest, lit the straw, smoked out the bees, put out the fire, and set to work eating the honey.

In the midst of the feast, who should appear at the foot of the tree but Sim'ba, the lion? Looking up, and seeing them eating, he asked, "Who are you?"

Then Soongoora whispered to Bookoo, "Hold your tongue; that old fellow is crazy." But in a very little while Simba roared out angrily: "Who are you, I say? Speak, I tell you!" This made Bookoo so scared that he blurted out, "It's only us!"

Upon this the hare said to him: "You just wrap me up in this straw, call to the lion to keep out of the way, and then throw me down. Then you'll see what will happen."

So Bookoo, the big rat, wrapped Soongoora, the hare, in the straw, and then called to Simba, the lion, "Stand back; I'm going to throw this straw down, and then I'll come down myself." When Simba stepped back out of the way, Bookoo threw down the straw, and as it lay on the ground Soongoora crept out and ran away while the lion was looking up.

After waiting a minute or two, Simba roared out, "Well, come down, I say!" and, there being no help for it, the big rat came down.

As soon as he was within reach, the lion caught hold of him, and asked, "Who was up there with you?"

"Why," said Bookoo, "Soongoora, the hare. Didn't you see him when I threw him down?"

"Of course I didn't see him," replied the lion, in an incredulous tone, and, without wasting further time, he ate the big rat, and then searched around for the hare, but could not find him.

Three days later, Soongoora called on his acquaintance, Kobay, the tortoise, and said to him, "Let us go and eat some honey."

"Whose honey?" inquired Kobay, cautiously.

"My father's," Soongoora replied.

"Oh, all right; I'm with you," said the tortoise, eagerly; and away they went.

When they arrived at the great calabash tree they climbed up with their straw, smoked out the bees, sat down, and began to eat.

Just then Mr. Simba, who owned the honey, came out again, and, looking up, inquired, "Who are you, up there?"

Soongoora whispered to Kobay, "Keep quiet;" but when the lion repeated his question angrily, Kobay became suspicious, and said: "I *will* speak. You told me this honey was yours; am I right in suspecting that it belongs to Simba?"

So, when the lion asked again, "Who are you?" he answered, "It's only us." The lion said, "Come down, then;" and the tortoise answered, "We're coming."

Now, Simba had been keeping an eye open for Soongoora since the day he caught Bookoo, the big rat, and, suspecting that he was up there with Kobay, he said to himself, "I've got him this time, sure."

Seeing that they were caught again, Soongoora said to the tortoise: "Wrap me up in the straw, tell Sim'ba to stand out of the way, and then throw me down. I'll wait for you below. He can't hurt you, you know."

"All right," said Kobay; but while he was wrapping the hare up he said to himself: "This fellow wants to run away, and leave me to bear the lion's anger. He shall get caught first." Therefore, when he had bundled him up, he called out, "Soongoora is coming!" and threw him down.

So Simba caught the hare, and, holding him with his paw, said, "Now, what shall I do with you?" The hare replied, "It's of no use for you to try to eat me; I'm awfully tough." "What would be the best thing to do with you, then?" asked Simba.

"I think," said Soongoora, "you should take me by the tail, whirl me around, and knock me against the ground. Then you may be able to eat me."

So the lion, being deceived, took him by the tail and whirled him around, but just as he was going to knock him on the ground he slipped out of his grasp and ran away, and Simba had the mortification of losing him again.

Angry and disappointed, he turned to the tree and called to Kobay, "You come down, too."

When the tortoise reached the ground, the lion said, "You're pretty hard; what can I do to make you eatable?"

"Oh, that's easy," laughed Kobay; "just put me in the mud and rub my back with your paw until my shell comes off."

Immediately on hearing this, Simba carried Kobay to the water, placed him in the mud, and began, as he supposed, to rub his back; but the tortoise had slipped away, and the lion continued rubbing on a piece of rock until his paws were raw. When he glanced down at them he saw they were bleeding, and, realizing that he had again been outwitted, he said, "Well, the hare has done me to-day, but I'll go hunting now until I find him."

So Simba, the lion, set out immediately in search of Soongoora, the hare, and as he went along he inquired of every one he met, "Where is the house of Soongoora?" But each person he asked answered, "I do not know." For the hare had said to his wife, "Let us remove from this house." Therefore the folks in that neighborhood had no knowledge of his whereabouts. Simba, however, went along, continuing his inquiries, until presently one answered, "That is his house on the top of the mountain."

Without loss of time the lion climbed the mountain, and soon arrived at the place indicated, only to find that there was no one at home. This, however, did not trouble him; on the contrary, saying to himself, "I'll hide myself inside, and when Soongoora and his wife come home I'll eat them both," he entered the house and lay down, awaiting their arrival.

Pretty soon along came the hare with his wife, not thinking of any danger; but he very soon discovered the marks of the lion's paws on the steep path. Stopping at once, he said to Mrs. Soongoora: "You go back, my dear. Simba, the lion, has passed this way, and I think he must be looking for me."

But she replied, "I will not go back; I will follow you, my husband."

Although greatly pleased at this proof of his wife's affection, Soongoora said firmly: "No, no; you have friends to go to. Go back."

So he persuaded her, and she went back; but he kept on, following the foot-marks, and saw—as he had suspected—that they went into his house.

"Ah!" said he to himself, "Mr. Lion is inside, is he?" Then, cautiously going back a little way, he called out: "How d'ye do, house? How d'ye do?" Waiting a moment, he remarked loudly: "Well, this is very strange! Every day, as I pass this place, I say, 'How d'ye do, house?' and the house always answers, 'How d'ye do?' There must be some one inside to-day."

When the lion heard this he called out, "How d'ye do?"

Then Soongoora burst out laughing, and shouted: "Oho, Mr. Simba! *You're* inside, and I'll bet you want to eat *me*; but first tell me where you ever heard of a house talking!"

Upon this the lion, seeing how he had been fooled, replied angrily, "You wait until I get hold of you; that's all."

"Oh, I think *you'll* have to do the waiting," cried the hare; and then he ran away, the lion following.

But it was of no use. Soongoora completely tired out old Simba, who, saying, "That rascal has beaten me; I don't want to have anything more to do with him," returned to his home under the great calabash tree.

THE MONKEY,
the SHARK, and the
WASHERMAN'S DONKEY

Tanzania

Once upon a time Kee'ma, the monkey, and Pa'pa, the shark, became great friends. The monkey lived in an immense mkooyoo tree which grew by the margin of the sea—half of its branches being over the water and half over the land.

Every morning, when the monkey was breakfasting on the kooyoo nuts, the shark would put in an appearance under the tree and call out, "Throw me some food, my friend;" with which request the monkey complied most willingly.

This continued for many months, until one day Papa said, "Keema, you have done me many kindnesses: I would like you to go with me to my home, that I may repay you."

"How can I go?" said the monkey; "we land beasts can not go about in the water."

"Don't trouble yourself about that," replied the shark; "I will carry you. Not a drop of water shall get to you."

"Oh, all right, then," said Mr. Keema; "let's go."

When they had gone about half-way the shark stopped, and said: "You are my friend. I will tell you the truth."

"Why, what is there to tell?" asked the monkey, with surprise.

"Well, you see, the fact is that our sultan is very sick, and we have been told that the only medicine that will do him any good is a monkey's heart."

"Well," exclaimed Keema, "you were very foolish not to tell me that before we started!"

"How so?" asked Papa.

But the monkey was busy thinking up some means of saving himself, and made no reply.

"Well?" said the shark, anxiously; "why don't you speak?"

"Oh, I've nothing to say now. It's too late. But if you had told me this before we started, I might have brought my heart with me."

"What? haven't you your heart here?"

"Huh!" ejaculated Keema; "don't you know about us? When we go out we leave our hearts in the trees, and go about with only our bodies. But I see you don't believe me. You think I'm scared. Come on; let's go to your home, where you can kill me and search for my heart in vain."

The shark did believe him, though, and exclaimed, "Oh, no; let's go back and get your heart."

"Indeed, no," protested Keema; "let us go on to your home."

But the shark insisted that they should go back, get the heart, and start afresh.

At last, with great apparent reluctance, the monkey consented, grumbling sulkily at the unnecessary trouble he was being put to.

When they got back to the tree, he climbed up in a great hurry, calling out, "Wait there, Papa, my friend, while I get my heart, and we'll start off properly next time."

When he had got well up among the branches, he sat down and kept quite still.

After waiting what he considered a reasonable length of time, the shark called, "Come along, Keema!" But Keema just kept still and said nothing.

In a little while he called again: "Oh, Keema! let's be going."

At this the monkey poked his head out from among the upper branches and asked, in great surprise, "Going? Where?"

"To my home, of course."

"Are you mad?" queried Keema.

"Mad? Why, what do you mean?" cried Papa.

"What's the matter with you?" said the monkey. "Do you take me for a washerman's donkey?"

"What peculiarity is there about a washerman's donkey?"

"It is a creature that has neither heart nor ears."

The shark, his curiosity overcoming his haste, thereupon begged to be told the story of the washerman's donkey, which the monkey related as follows:

"A washerman owned a donkey, of which he was very fond. One day, however, it ran away, and took up its abode in the forest, where it led a lazy life, and consequently grew very fat.

"At length Soongoo'ra, the hare, by chance passed that way, and saw Poon'da, the donkey.

"Now, the hare is the most cunning of all beasts—if you look at his mouth you will see that he is always talking to himself about everything.

"So when Soongoora saw Poonda he said to himself, 'My, this donkey is fat!' Then he went and told Simba, the lion.

"As Simba was just recovering from a severe illness, he was still so weak that he could not go hunting. He was consequently pretty hungry.

"Said Mr. Soongoora, 'I'll bring enough meat to-morrow for both of us to have a great feast, but you'll have to do the killing.'

"'All right, good friend,' exclaimed Simba, joyfully; 'you're very kind.'

"So the hare scampered off to the forest, found the donkey, and said to her, in his most courtly manner, 'Miss Poonda, I am sent to ask your hand in marriage.'

"'By whom?' simpered the donkey.

"'By Simba, the lion.'

"The donkey was greatly elated at this, and exclaimed: 'Let's go at once. This is a first-class offer.'

"They soon arrived at the lion's home, were cordially invited in, and sat down. Soongoora gave Simba a signal with his eyebrow, to the effect that this was the promised feast, and that he would wait outside. Then he said to Poonda: 'I must leave you for a while to attend to some private business. You stay here and converse with your husband that is to be.'

"As soon as Soongoora got outside, the lion sprang at Poonda, and they had a great fight. Simba was kicked very hard, and he struck with his claws as well as his weak health would permit him. At last the donkey threw the lion down, and ran away to her home in the forest.

"Shortly after, the hare came back, and called, 'Haya! Simba! have you got it?'

"'I have not got it,' growled the lion; 'she kicked me and ran away; but I warrant you I made her feel pretty sore, though I'm not strong.'

"'Oh, well,' remarked Soongoora; 'don't put yourself out of the way about it.'

"Then Soongoora waited many days, until the lion and the donkey were both well and strong, when he said: 'What do you think now, Simba? Shall I bring you your meat?'

"'Ay,' growled the lion, fiercely; 'bring it to me. I'll tear it in two pieces!'

"So the hare went off to the forest, where the donkey welcomed him and asked the news.

"'You are invited to call again and see your lover,' said Soongoora.

"'Oh, dear!' cried Poonda; 'that day you took me to him he scratched me awfully. I'm afraid to go near him now.'

"'Ah, pshaw!' said Soongoora; 'that's nothing. That's only Simba's way of caressing.'

"'Oh, well,' said the donkey, 'let's go.'

"So off they started again; but as soon as the lion caught sight of Poonda he sprang upon her and tore her in two pieces.

"When the hare came up, Simba said to him: 'Take this meat and roast it. As for myself, all I want is the heart and ears.'

"'Thanks,' said Soongoora. Then he went away and roasted the meat in a place where the lion could not see him, and he took the heart and ears and hid them. Then he ate all the meat he needed, and put the rest away.

"Presently the lion came to him and said, 'Bring me the heart and ears.'

"'Where are they?' said the hare.

"'What does this mean?' growled Simba.

"'Why, didn't you know this was a washerman's donkey?'

"'Well, what's that to do with there being no heart or ears?'

"'For goodness' sake, Simba, aren't you old enough to know that if this beast had possessed a heart and ears it wouldn't have come back the second time?'

"Of course the lion had to admit that what Soongoora, the hare, said was true.

"And now," said Keema to the shark, "you want to make a washerman's donkey of me. Get out of there, and go home by yourself. You are not going to get me again, and our friendship is ended. Good-bye, Papa."

THE STORY of the HARE, KI-KAMBA-WA-PARUKU or BUKU

Kenya (Kamba)

There once was a time when the hare was very poor, but he was ambitious and anxious to become rich, and one day he went for a walk in the woods, and stopping to rest fell asleep. When he awoke from his sleep he espied some cattle, sheep and goats near by, and he said to himself, "I will creep up quietly, and I shall be able to get some milk," so he slipped stealthily through the grass and sucked some milk from a cow; he then looked round to see who was herding the animals, and he saw a MuKamba asleep under a tree; so he there and then collected the grazing beasts and drove them away into the heart of the woods. He then took a knife and cut off the animals' tails and took them back to a native path which passed near where the herdsman was sleeping; this path was split up into three parallel trails, and in one of these he buried the tails of the cattle in a row, and in the next one he planted a row of sheep's tails and in the third one he planted a row of goats' tails: he planted them all with the tip of the tail protruding above ground.

The hare then approached the drowsy herdsman and called out, "*Nthi Nthi Kumeseo*" which means "The earth has eaten up your property." The MuKamba awoke with a start and looked around in vain for his live-stock. The hare then hopped out of a bush, called the man and told him to follow him. The herdsman did so, and the hare took him along the path to the place where the tails were sticking out of the ground and said, "See, the earth has swallowed up everything but the tips of their tails, but let us pull both together at the tails and drag back your animals." The herdsman agreed to this, and the hare instructed him to pull when he gave the word, and when the MuKamba pulled upwards at a tail the hare pushed downwards as hard as the MuKamba pulled upwards, so the tails would not move; presently the hare suddenly loosed hold and the tail came away in the MuKamba's hand, and the hare cried out, "Oh! it has broken off and left the beast below ground"; they then went on to where the sheep's tails were buried and then on to the goats' tails, and the same thing happened. The MuKamba then enquired what was next to be done, and the hare replied, "Well, the only thing is to dig out the animals, and so go and fetch a digging stick." The MuKamba did so, and dug a big hole without finding anything. The hare however still urged him to go on digging, that he would be sure to find them if he only dug deep enough. The man dug and dug until he was quite exhausted, and he then gave it up as a bad job. The hare said, "You seem to be too tired to dig any deeper, so you had better go back to your village, but when you get home what shall you tell your friends?" The man said, "I shall tell them that the earth has swallowed up my cattle and sheep."

So they parted, and the hare collected the live-stock and drove it off towards his home. On the way he met a lion, and the lion said, "How did a small person like you get all this wealth?" and the hare replied, "Oh! I have been on a raiding expedition and taken it by force, and I had to kill nine men to get it, and if you interfere with me I will kill you too." The lion was so taken aback by this boastful speech that he was afraid to tackle the hare alone, so he went off and called in a friend and said, "Come along and I will shew you where there is a lot of stock to be had for the taking," and he explained his meeting with the hare. The second lion expressed surprise at his requiring help, but the other replied, "That is so, but the owner is a fierce little beast; he has killed nine men in capturing the herd." The second lion however encouraged him and said, "Come along, let us both go and roar loudly at the hare and put on a fierce air, and we shall soon see if he really is the brave person he professes to be."

They did so, with the result that the hare was terrified and hid in a bush and called out, "*Mutwa Ubiu* (which is a nickname given to the lion by the hare), don't let us fight about this matter, but let us divide the spoil." The lion agreed, and they halved the live-stock.

The hare was exceedingly angry at losing half his spoil, and sat down to consider how he could get the better of the lion and encompass his death by stratagem. When he had thought out his plan he went to the lion and said, "Now our difference is finished let us eat *Kithito*" (*tule Kithito*, that is to say, "let us go through the peace ceremony together"). The lion agreed, and the hare said that to carry out the ceremony to which he was accustomed they must make a big fire, so he and the lion went and collected firewood and then lit a fire.

The hare then explained that they must both jump over the fire in turn, and he went back a little distance, took a run and jumped over the fire; the fire had at that time not yet burnt up properly. He then went and sat down by the fire and said to the lion, "I have run a thorn into my foot which I must pull out, but you now go on and jump the fire." The fire by this time had burnt up and was much fiercer. The lion came along with a run, and as he got close to the fire the hare picked up some hot ashes and threw them into his eyes, and so the lion jumped short, fell into the fire, and was burned to death.

The hare thus recovered his spoil and went off happily with his flocks and herds, and to this day the lion is so afraid of the hare that he is never known to kill and eat him. After a time however the herding of all his live-stock became a burden to the hare, so he eventually took it along and handed it over to a MuKamba and said, "Herd my property for me, and I will turn up now and again and drink milk." And so it is to this day, when cattle and goats are out grazing a hare will frequently come along and suckle the animals.

WOKUBIRA OMULALU MU KYAMA

Uganda (Baganda)

A very long time ago there was a King who called Walukaga, the chief of his smiths, and gave him a great quantity of iron and said: "I want you to make a real man for me, one who can walk and talk, and who has blood in his body, and who has brains." Walukaga took the iron and went home, but he was at a loss what to do, and no one could advise him how to set about making the real man. He went about among his friends telling them what the King had said, and asked what he had better do. No one was able to give him any advice; they all knew that the King would not accept anything short of an honest trial, and would punish the man for not carrying out his commands.

On the way home one day Walukaga met a former friend who had gone mad, and who lived alone on some waste land. Walukaga did not know he was mad until he met him. When they approached each other, Walukaga greeted his old friend, and the madman asked him where he had come from. Walukaga reasoned for a moment and then said to himself: "Why should I not tell him my story? Even though he is mad, he used to be my friend." So he answered: "I have come from some friends where I have been trying to get advice." The madman asked what advice he wanted, and Walukaga told him all the King had said, and the work he had given him to do, and how he had given him the iron, and then added: "What am I to do?" The madman answered: "If the King has told you to do this work go to him and say, that if he really wishes to have a nice man forged he is to order all the people to shave their heads and burn the hair until they have made up a thousand loads of charcoal, and he is to get one hundred large pots of water from the tears of the people with which to slake the fire and keep it from burning too fiercely."

Walukaga returned to the King and said to him: "My Lord, if you wish me to make this man quickly and well, order the people to shave their heads and burn the hair, and make a thousand loads of charcoal out of it for me to work the iron into the man. Further, make them collect a hundred pots full of tears to act as water for the work, because the charcoal from wood and the ordinary water from wells are of no use for forging a man."

The King agreed to the request and gave the order to all the people to shave their heads and burn the hair into charcoal, and to collect all the tears. When they had all shaved their heads and burnt their hair, there was not nearly one load of charcoal, and when they had collected all the tears there were not two pots full of water. When the King saw the results of his endeavours he sent for the smith Walukaga, and said to him: "Don't trouble to make the man, because I am unable to get the charcoal or the tears for the water." Walukaga knelt down and thanked the King; he then added, "My Lord, it was because I knew you would be unable to get the hair for charcoal and the tears for the water that I asked for them; you had asked me to do an impossible thing." All the people present laughed and said: "Walukaga speaks the truth."

THE CAT and the FOWL

✺

Uganda (Baganda)

At one time the fowls used to be lords of the wild cats, and made them their servants and employed them to supply them with food. Whenever a cat caught flying ants, the fowls demanded four-fifths of all they caught; this tax was paid in large packets of ants, which the cats had to tie up and bring before the fowls to let them see what spoil they had taken. The cats did not like this arrangement, and once or twice they wished to rebel, but were cowed by the fowls threatening to burn them with their combs.

One day the cats' fire had gone out, and a mother cat sent one of the younger members of the family to the fowls to beg for fire. When the young cat arrived, he found the Cock very drunk and fast asleep, and the others away from home; he tried to wake him, but failed to do so; he therefore went back and told his mother. The mother said: "Go back again with some dry grass and put it to his comb and bring the fire"; so he went back and applied the grass to the comb, but there was no fire.

The young cat returned to his mother and told her the grass would not take fire; the mother was angry and said, "You have not really tried, come along with me and do it again." When they went again, the cock was still asleep. They approached him very slowly, and touched the comb with the grass, and then blew on it to see if it was on fire, but there was never a spark; they felt if the comb was hot, putting their hands gently on it, though they were dreadfully afraid of being burnt.

To their great surprise they found that the comb was quite cold, even though it was red; after feeling it they finally waked the fowl and told him they were not going to serve him any longer, they were tired of his rule.

The fowl was angry and began to make a great noise, and tried to terrify the cats with threats, but they said, "We don't fear you; we have tested your comb while you were asleep and know that it has no fire in it, and now we will kill you if you say anything more." The fowl saw that his empty boasting had been discovered, and from that time fowls have had to escape cats because of the enmity between them; for this reason fowls took refuge with man to be safe from cats.

THE STORY of the NGU or TORTOISE and the KIPALALA or FISH EAGLE

Kenya (Kamba)

An old Mu-Kamba had a very comely daughter, and the tortoise came along and made her father an offer of marriage, and the eagle also sought the girl in marriage. To both these suitors the father replied, "The one who wins my daughter must start at daybreak for the coast and return to me before nightfall with some sea salt."

And the eagle said to the tortoise, "Then of course the prize is mine, for you who only move at a snail's pace will never accomplish this task." The tortoise replied, "It is truly very difficult for me, but promise me one thing—agree to put off the contest for 10 months," and the eagle, feeling quite sure of winning, agreed to do so.

Next day, unknown to the eagle, he started off for the coast to fetch some salt; it took him nearly five months to go and five to return, and he hid the salt in his house. Now during his journey to the coast he arranged with all the tortoises he met on the way to station themselves on a certain day at intervals along the route between Ukamba and the coast, one at each of the various camps, streams and water-holes, and he told them all to look out for the eagle as he flew past on the appointed day and when the eagle called out, *"Ngu iko"* ("Tortoise, are you there?"), each one was to reply in turn, *"Ni iko"* ("I am here"). On the appointed day the eagle started off on his flight to the sea and at intervals he called out, *"Ngu iko,"* and at various points *en route* he received the arranged reply. He was very surprised to find the tortoise getting on so quickly, and still more so when he reached the shore and found a tortoise there in the act of collecting some salt. He however quickly picked up his own salt and flew back at full speed, and not knowing that the tortoise he had left on the beach was not his competitor, felt confident he had won. About 4 o'clock in the afternoon the original tortoise, who was on the look out, saw the eagle like a speck in the distance, so he emerged from where he had hidden throughout the day and waddled up the road to the village, announced his return from the coast and handed his packet of salt to the girl's father.

The eagle then arrived and was very surprised and annoyed to find that he had been outwitted by the tortoise. The old MuKamba suspected some trick and said to the eagle, "When you reached the coast did you see the tortoise?" and the eagle said, "Yes, but I cannot think how he has managed to get here before me," and he was very angry and flew off in a great temper.

And the old man said, "It is true you have won, but if I give you my daughter where will you live in safety, for the eagle is so angry that he is sure to find you out and kill you." The tortoise replied, "Oh! that is all right, do not be anxious for my safety, my home will in future be in the water and the eagle will never get me." So he took the girl and dived into the water, and this is the origin of the tortoise spending a great part of his life in the water, which it does to this day.

KIWOBE AND HIS SHEEP

Uganda (Baganda)

Once upon a time there was a man named Kiwobe who had a sheep, and an only son named Kakange. One day Kiwobe went out to visit a friend, and the sheep said to the boy Kakange: "Kiwobe said when you saw the sun shining you were to take me out to the pasture; what are you doing? Are you waiting until it is evening to take me out?" When the man returned home, his son told him what the sheep had said. Kiwobe said, "My child, why do you tell lies? Can a sheep talk like a man?" The boy said: "If you think I am telling you lies, pretend you are going away, and after going a little distance, turn back and hide near the door and listen, and you will hear it speak." Kiwobe did as the boy had suggested; he hid near the house, and after a short time the sheep called to the boy and asked: "What did Kiwobe tell you?" The boy replied: "He said, 'When you see the sun shining untie the sheep, and take it out to the pasture.'" The sheep said, "Well, what do you see now?"

When Kiwobe heard it, he went and told his companions, saying he was at a loss what to do because his sheep spoke like a man. His companions advised him to cut a palm-pole, bring it, and drop it upon the sheep and kill it. Kiwobe brought the pole as they suggested, and dropped it by the sheep; the sheep, however, sprang aside and escaped, and said to Kiwobe, "Do you want to kill me? I will not blame you this time, because you are tired."

When Kiwobe saw he had failed to kill the sheep he left the place secretly, and went to live elsewhere leaving the sheep tied in the house; he had also forgotten to take with him his axe-handle. The sheep took the axe-handle and followed the man along the road and found him at a dance. It said to the people dancing, "What kind of a dance is this?" and at once began to dance and sing: "This is coming, yes, but not arrived; this is coming, yes, but not arrived." As it was dancing it saw its master Kiwobe, and went to him and said, "My brother, why did you leave me in the house? you also left your axe-handle which I have brought." All the people at the dance were greatly surprised to hear the sheep speak, but Kiwobe fled away and the sheep ran after him, and they both arrived together at the house.

Kiwobe then agreed with his wife that she should kill the sheep when he went away for a walk. The sheep, however, overheard the man tell his wife to kill it, and when Kiwobe had gone it caught the woman and killed her. It then cut her up and cooked her, and took her clothes and put them on. When Kiwobe returned he asked his wife if she had killed the sheep, and it replied, "Yes; and I am cooking it now." Kiwobe said, "Dish up the food," and the sheep did so, and the man sat down to eat his meal. When Kiwobe was eating his son came up and said to him, "Sir, that which brings your food is the sheep, it has killed your wife and cooked her." When Kiwobe heard this he rose up, and got his spear to kill the sheep, but it fled away and escaped during the night. This is the reason why women never eat mutton.

MONSTERS
AND MAGIC

THE STORY of M'WAMBÍA and the N'JENGÉ

Told by N'jár-Ge, son of the Chief Mungé
Kenya (Kikuyu)

Once upon a time there was a man who married a wife, and she bore him a male child; and he married a second wife, and she also bore him a male child. And after a while the first wife died. Now the name of the eldest son was M'wambía, and the name of the second was also M'wambía, and he was known as M'wambía the Less, to distinguish him from his brother.

Now when the two boys were about twelve and ten years, it happened that the animal known as N'Jengé came from the wilds, and ate the food in the fields; so the two brothers went into the woods, and M'wambía the Elder made a snare to catch the N'Jengé, and M'wambía the Less also made a snare at a little distance away. Now an N'Jengé came into the snare of M'wambía the Less, and he released it and killed it and ate it. And an N'Jengé also came into the snare of M'wambía the Elder, but he released it and did not kill it; he let it go free into the woods, and the two boys returned to the village and said nothing to their father.

Now the mother of M'wambía the Less went into the fields and gathered sugar-cane, and put it into her basket on her back and brought it to the house, and the father took a large piece and gave it to his elder son, but to the younger he gave a small piece; and the younger said, "Why have you given me a small piece and my brother a big piece?" And he said, "Because you have a mother, while the mother of your brother is dead." Then M'wambía the Less said to his father, "Come into the woods"; and he showed him the two snares, and told him how he had killed the N'Jengé which he had caught, and how M'wambía the Elder had let his go.

And the father was very angry and upbraided his elder son, because the N'Jengé was very fat, and he chose a tree, tall, with a straight stem, and made him climb up it, and then he took sticks and stuck them into the ground around the tree with the points leaning inwards towards the tree, and made the points sharp, so that if the boy descended or fell down, the points would run into him and he would die; and he went away and left M'wambía in the tree.

Now M'wambía stayed in the tree for twenty days, and at the end of that time an N'Jengé came and said, "Man'-gi[1] Ki-hú-ti[2]!" And M'wambía said, "I am not Mangi, I am M'wambía." And the N'Jengé took one spike and carried it away, and ten N'Jengé came and each took one spike and carried it away; and at last the N'Jengé came whom M'wambía had set free, and he said, "Mangi." And he said, "I am M'wambía," and he told him how he had set him free. And the N'Jengé, when he heard this, carried away all the remaining spikes; and M'wambía gradually unloosed the grip of his arms around the stem of the tree, and slid to the bottom. And the N'Jengé made a hole open in his side, and out came a big sheep. M'wambía took some fat to eat; and at first he could not eat it for he was so weak, and was very sick; but afterwards he ate a little, and then a little of the leg, and then next day he ate another leg, and the sheep lasted him for food four days; and at the end of that time the N'Jengé opened his side again and there came out a goat, and that lasted for food four days, and then there came out two goats, and these lasted three days, for M'wambía had grown stronger and bigger; and there then came an ox, and the N'Jengé ate too, and M'wambía grew still bigger and stronger, and the N'Jengé said, "Go amongst the long grass and jump," And M'wambía went amongst the long grass and jumped twice, and N'Jengé said, "You are not yet strong enough"; and they ate another ox, and then he said, "Go and jump again"; and he went and jumped four times. And he said to him, "What would you like to possess?" And he said, "A goat." And the N'Jengé opened his side and gave him one hundred female goats which had not borne, one hundred female goats which had borne, one hundred young goats who knew their mother, one hundred male goats, one hundred fat male goats, one hundred sheep which had not borne,

---

1. No meaning could be found—is simply a name.
2. Tree or bush.

one hundred sheep which had borne, one hundred young sheep who knew their mother, one hundred male sheep, one hundred fat male sheep, one hundred cows which had not borne, one hundred cows which had borne, one hundred calves, one hundred oxen, one hundred fat oxen.

And the N'Jengé said to M'wambía again, "What do you want?" And M'wambía replied, "Women."

And the N'Jengé gave him two hundred goats and two hundred oxen to buy women; and M'wambía bought one hundred women. And the N'Jengé said again, "What do you want" And he said, "I want nothing more."

Then he went to the Gura river, and he built a big village for his wives and his oxen and his goats. But no children were yet born, so M'wambía went and tended the goats, and he sat on a hillside where he could see them all, for they were many.

Now the mother of M'wambía the Less said to her young daughter, "Take a bag and go and get vegetables." So the child went to get the vegetables, but could see none; and she walked and walked, and at last she saw M'wambía sitting on the hillside herding goats, and she called out, "That is our M'wambía who was lost." And he said nothing. And then she called out again, "That is our M'wambía who was lost." So he spoke to her, and he asked, "How are they all at home, my father and my father's brother?" She said, "They are well"; and she saw his village and his wives and cattle; and he took a goat and killed it and cut it up and put it into her bag. She walked twelve hours, and came to her home. As she came to the homestead she called out to her mother, "Bring me the cooking-pot to cook the vegetables." And her mother brought a little one, and she said, "Bring me a big one." And she brought a bigger, and the girl said, "That is not big enough." And the mother said, "Do you want the one in which we cook meat?" and she said, "Yes." And she said, "What kind of vegetables have you got that you want so large a pot?" The mother opened the bag and saw the meat, and she said, "You have stolen a goat." And she said, "I have not stolen it; it is from M'wambía." And she said, "Do not tell a lie. M'wambía is lost." And the girl said, "I have seen him, and the day after to-morrow you shall come and see him too." And she told how she had seen him and his many goods. So the next day they cooked the meat and ate it, and the day after they all went together to see M'wambía, his father and his father's brother, and the mother and the father's other wife, and M'wambía the Less and the girl, and all the family. And when they came to where M'wambía was, they saw him sitting on the hill herding goats; and there was a river between, and M'wambía took a string and he tied a goat to the end of the string, and threw it across the river. And the father took hold of it to go to M'wambía; and as he was being pulled across the river he was drowned, because he had been cruel to his son. But the others got across safely, and when they came to the village of M'wambía and saw his many goods, they stayed there and made their home with him. And after a while M'wambía said, "I have many men and women in my homestead who do work." And he gave his relations work to do; one to mind the goats, one to mind the young goats, and one to work in the fields. And he said, "I will go away for a while and see if they do their work well." And he went to another village and there slept for five days. And when he came back to his homestead he saw some fat, and he said, "What is this fat on the ground?" And he looked and saw on the wall the head of N'Jengé, and he knew that his friend the N'Jengé had come to the village while he was away, and his relatives had killed it. And he said no word to them, but he said to himself, "My luck is gone, because the N'Jengé is dead with whom I am of one heart." And he took a stone and a knife and made his knife very sharp, and he killed all the women and all the men, and all the goats and all the cattle, and then he took the knife and plunged it in his own breast, for the N'Jengé was dead.

THE MAGICIAN
and the SULTAN'S SON

❦

Tanzania

There was once a sultan who had three little sons, and no one seemed to be able to teach them anything; which greatly grieved both the sultan and his wife.

One day a magician came to the sultan and said, "If I take your three boys and teach them to read and write, and make great scholars of them, what will you give me?"

And the sultan said, "I will give you half of my property."

"No," said the magician; "that won't do."

"I'll give you half of the towns I own."

"No; that will not satisfy me."

"What do you want, then?"

"When I have made them scholars and bring them back to you, choose two of them for yourself and give me the third; for I want to have a companion of my own."

"Agreed," said the sultan.

So the magician took them away, and in a remarkably short time taught them to read, and to make letters, and made them quite good scholars. Then he took them back to the sultan and said: "Here are the children. They are all equally good scholars. Choose."

So the sultan took the two he preferred, and the magician went away with the third, whose name was Keejaa'naa, to his own house, which was a very large one.

When they arrived, Mchaa'wee, the magician, gave the youth all the keys, saying, "Open whatever you wish to." Then he told him that he was his father, and that he was going away for a month.

When he was gone, Keejaanaa took the keys and went to examine the house. He opened one door, and saw a room full of liquid gold. He put his finger in, and the gold stuck to it, and, wipe and rub as he would, the gold would not come off; so he wrapped a piece of rag around it, and when his supposed father came home and saw the rag, and asked him what he had been doing to his finger, he was afraid to tell him the truth, so he said that he had cut it.

Not very long after, Mchaawee went away again, and the youth took the keys and continued his investigations.

The first room he opened was filled with the bones of goats, the next with sheep's bones, the next with the bones of oxen, the fourth with the bones of donkeys, the fifth with those of horses, the sixth contained men's skulls, and in the seventh was a live horse.

"Hullo!" said the horse; "where do you come from, you son of Adam?"

"This is my father's house," said Keejaanaa.

"Oh, indeed!" was the reply. "Well, you've got a pretty nice parent! Do you know that he occupies himself with eating people, and donkeys, and horses, and oxen and goats and everything he can lay his hands on? You and I are the only living things left."

This scared the youth pretty badly, and he faltered, "What are we to do?"

"What's your name?" said the horse.

"Keejaanaa."

"Well, I'm Faaraa'see. Now, Keejaanaa, first of all, come and unfasten me."

The youth did so at once.

"Now, then, open the door of the room with the gold in it, and I will swallow it all; then I'll go and wait for you under the big tree down the road a little way. When the magician comes home, he will say to you, 'Let us go for firewood;' then you answer, 'I don't understand that work;' and he will go by himself. When he comes back, he will put a great big pot on the hook and will tell you to make a fire under it. Tell him you don't know how to make a fire, and he will make it himself.

"Then he will bring a large quantity of butter, and while it is getting hot he will put up a swing and say to you, 'Get up there, and I'll swing you.' But you tell him you never played at that game, and ask him to swing first, that you may see how it is done. Then he will get up to show you; and you must push him into the big pot, and then come to me as quickly as you can."

Then the horse went away.

Now, Mchaawee had invited some of his friends to a feast at his house that evening; so, returning home early, he said to Keejaanaa, "Let us go for firewood;" but the youth answered, "I don't understand that work." So he went by himself and brought the wood.

Then he hung up the big pot and said, "Light the fire;" but the youth said, "I don't know how to do it." So the magician laid the wood under the pot and lighted it himself.

Then he said, "Put all that butter in the pot;" but the youth answered, "I can't lift it; I'm not strong enough." So he put in the butter himself.

Next Mchaawee said, "Have you seen our country game?" And Keejaanaa answered, "I think not."

"Well," said the magician, "let's play at it while the butter is getting hot."

So he tied up the swing and said to Keejaanaa, "Get up here, and learn the game." But the youth said: "You get up first and show me. I'll learn quicker that way."

The magician got into the swing, and just as he got started Keejaanaa gave him a push right into the big pot; and as the butter was by this time boiling, it not only killed him, but cooked him also.

As soon as the youth had pushed the magician into the big pot, he ran as fast as he could to the big tree, where the horse was waiting for him.

"Come on," said Faaraasee; "jump on my back and let's be going."

So he mounted and they started off.

When the magician's guests arrived they looked everywhere for him, but, of course, could not find him. Then, after waiting a while, they began to be very hungry; so, looking around for something to eat, they saw that the stew in the big pot was done, and, saying to each other, "Let's begin, anyway," they started in and ate the entire contents of the pot. After they had finished, they searched for Mchaawee again, and finding lots of provisions in the house, they thought they would stay there until he came; but after they had waited a couple of days and eaten all the food in the place, they gave him up and returned to their homes.

Meanwhile Keejaanaa and the horse continued on their way until they had gone a great distance, and at last they stopped near a large town.

"Let us stay here," said the youth, "and build a house."

As Faaraasee was agreeable, they did so. The horse coughed up all the gold he had swallowed, with which they purchased slaves, and cattle, and everything they needed.

When the people of the town saw the beautiful new house and all the slaves, and cattle, and riches it contained, they went and told their sultan, who at once made up his mind that the owner of such a place must be of sufficient importance to be visited and taken notice of, as an acquisition to the neighborhood.

So he called on Keejaanaa, and inquired who he was.

"Oh, I'm just an ordinary being, like other people."

"Are you a traveler?"

"Well, I have been; but I like this place, and think I'll settle down here."

"Why don't you come and walk in our town?"

"I should like to very much, but I need some one to show me around."

"Oh, I'll show you around," said the sultan, eagerly, for he was quite taken with the young man.

After this Keejaanaa and the sultan became great friends; and in the course of time the young man married the sultan's daughter, and they had one son.

They lived very happily together, and Keejaanaa loved Faaraasee as his own soul.

THE STORY of the GIRL WHO CUT the HAIR of the N'JENGÉ

Told by Kar-an'-ja, a young M'kikúyu
Kenya (Kikuyu)

nce upon a time a young warrior sent his little sister to fetch water from the river, and in bringing the water she let the gourd fall and broke it, and her brother was very angry, and said, "You have broken the gourd; go away and bring me back instead of it the hair of the N'Jengé." And the little girl ran away a long distance, for she was afraid her brother would beat her, and in the road she met an N'Jengé. He was very big and his hair was very long, and he was called I-lí-mu.

And when they got to the house of the N'Jengé he took a stick and struck with it on the ground, and a hole opened, and out of it came many cows and goats, and the girl ate; and then the N'Jengé struck again, and the rest of the cows and goats all vanished. And the same thing happened again, and she ate yet more, and became big and fat. Then the N'Jengé left home and went away on a journey. Now the N'Jengé had a child—a boy; and the boy loved the little girl dearly, and when his father was gone he said to her, "Give me your ornaments." And she took off the beads she wore round her neck and arms and gave them to him, and he put them on one side; and then he took a strong-smelling stuff and plastered it all over her neck and head, and said, "Now fly, for my father has gone to collect firewood to make a fire, and when he comes back he will eat you."

And the girl fled from the house of the N'Jengé. Now Ilímu had collected two friends, N'Jengé like himself, and they had all gone to get firewood to make a fire and have a great feast and eat the girl, and as she fled she met on the road the first of these bad N'Jengé carrying a bundle of sticks towards the house, and he said to her, "Are you the little girl of the N'Jengé?" And she said, "No, that little girl had armlets and bracelets." And he let her go on, and then she met the next friend and the same thing happened again; and last of all she met Ilímu himself, and he looked at her to see if she was the child he had caught, and he saw that she had no necklace and no armlets; and he came near and smelt the strong-smelling stuff, and he was persuaded that it was not the same girl, and he said to her, "I want some one to shave my beard and cut my hair." For he had a long beard and long hair behind. So she shaved his beard and cut his hair, and put the hair she cut off in her bag and went on her way, and came back to her mother's house.

When she came to her home she saw her brother who had been so angry with her, and gave him the hair of the N'Jengé as he had asked; but not long afterwards a young warrior came to buy the girl for his wife, and he gave the purchase money to her mother, thirty goats, and she went away with him to his house, for she loved him. But before she went she said to her mother, "Don't give my eldest brother the goats, for he has behaved cruelly to me, but keep them and let my younger brother have them," for her mother had also given birth to another boy, and she was fond of the child, but her other brother she did not love. And when the girl was gone the eldest brother came to the mother and said, "Give me the goats"; and the mother said, "No, I shall not give them to you, for they were paid as the marli of your sister, and she said you were not to have them, for you were angry with her because she had broken the gourd and told her she must go and get the hair of the N'Jengé." So the eldest brother went away, and the younger brother had the goats.

Now when the N'Jengé and his friends got to the house of Ilímu, they found that the girl had fled, and only the boy was there; and Ilímu feared greatly, for he said, "I have brought these friends to my home to eat, and there is the firewood, but there is no meat." And he took the two friends to a little distance, and the firewood, and told them to wait there, and he went back to the house and said to his son, "Run, boy, run and hide in the long grass." And Ilímu went into the house and dug a big hole in the floor and got a large stone, and got into the big hole and hid there, and drew the big stone to cover his head.

Now when the friends saw that he did not come back they went to look for him, and they called him and he did not answer, so one of them went inside the hut, found the great stone, and moved it and saw the head of Ilímu, and said, "Why did you not answer when we called?" And they took him out, one N'Jengé on each side, for they were two and he was one, and they got more firewood and built an enormous fire, and they roasted him and ate him, and that was the end of the bad N'Jengé.

MKAAAH JEECHONEE, the BOY HUNTER

Tanzania

Sultan Maaj'noon had seven sons and a big cat, of all of whom he was very proud.

Everything went well until one day the cat went and caught a calf. When they told the sultan he said, "Well, the cat is mine, and the calf is mine." So they said, "Oh, all right, master," and let the matter drop.

A few days later the cat caught a goat; and when they told the sultan he said, "The cat is mine, and the goat is mine;" and so that settled it again.

Two days more passed, and the cat caught a cow. They told the sultan, and he shut them up with "My cat, and my cow."

After another two days the cat caught a donkey; same result.

Next it caught a horse; same result.

The next victim was a camel; and when they told the sultan he said: "What's the matter with you folks? It was my cat, and my camel. I believe you don't like my cat, and want it killed, bringing me tales about it every day. Let it eat whatever it wants to."

In a very short time it caught a child, and then a full-grown man; but each time the sultan remarked that both the cat and its victim were his, and thought no more of it.

Meantime the cat grew bolder, and hung around a low, open place near the town, pouncing on people going for water, or animals out at pasture, and eating them.

At last some of the people plucked up courage; and, going to the sultan, said: "How is this, master? As you are our sultan you are our protector,—or ought to be,—yet you have allowed this cat to do as it pleases, and now it lives just out of town there, and kills everything living that goes that way, while at night it comes into town and does the same thing. Now, what on earth are we to do?"

But Maajnoon only replied: "I really believe you hate my cat. I suppose you want me to kill it; but I shall do no such thing. Everything it eats is mine."

Of course the folks were astonished at this result of the interview, and, as no one dared to kill the cat, they all had to remove from the vicinity where it lived. But this did not mend matters, because, when it found no one came that way, it shifted its quarters likewise.

So complaints continued to pour in, until at last Sultan Maajnoon gave orders that if any one came to make accusations against the cat, he was to be informed that the master could not be seen.

When things got so that people neither let their animals out nor went out themselves, the cat went farther into the country, killing and eating cattle, and fowls, and everything that came its way.

One day the sultan said to six of his sons, "I'm going to look at the country to-day; come along with me."

The seventh son was considered too young to go around anywhere, and was always left at home with the women folk, being called by his brothers Mkaa'ah Jeecho'nee, which means Mr. Sit-in-the-kitchen.

Well, they went, and presently came to a thicket. The father was in front and the six sons following him, when the cat jumped out and killed three of the latter.

The attendants shouted, "The cat! the cat!" and the soldiers asked permission to search for and kill it, which the sultan readily granted, saying: "This is not a cat, it is a noon'dah. It has taken from me my own sons."

Now, nobody had ever seen a noondah, but they all knew it was a terrible beast that could kill and eat all other living things.

When the sultan began to bemoan the loss of his sons, some of those who heard him said: "Ah, master, this noondah does not select his prey. He doesn't say: 'This is my master's son, I'll leave him alone,' or, 'This is my master's wife, I won't eat her.'

When we told you what the cat had done, you always said it was your cat, and what it ate was yours, and now it has killed your sons, and we don't believe it would hesitate to eat even you."

And he said, "I fear you are right."

As for the soldiers who tried to get the cat, some were killed and the remainder ran away, and the sultan and his living sons took the dead bodies home and buried them.

Now when Mkaaah Jeechonee, the seventh son, heard that his brothers had been killed by the noondah, he said to his mother, "I, too, will go, that it may kill me as well as my brothers, or I will kill it."

But his mother said: "My son, I do not like to have you go. Those three are already dead; and if you are killed also, will not that be one wound upon another to my heart?"

"Nevertheless," said he, "I can not help going; but do not tell my father."

So his mother made him some cakes, and sent some attendants with him; and he took a great spear, as sharp as a razor, and a sword, bade her farewell, and departed.

As he had always been left at home, he had no very clear idea what he was going to hunt for; so he had not gone far beyond the suburbs, when, seeing a very large dog, he concluded that this was the animal he was after; so he killed it, tied a rope to it, and dragged it home, singing,

> "Oh, mother, I have killed
> The noondah, eater of the people."

When his mother, who was upstairs, heard him, she looked out of the window, and, seeing what he had brought, said, "My son, this is not the noondah, eater of the people."

So he left the carcass outside and went in to talk about it, and his mother said, "My dear boy, the noondah is a much larger animal than that; but if I were you, I'd give the business up and stay at home."

"No, indeed," he exclaimed; "no staying at home for me until I have met and fought the noondah."

So he set out again, and went a great deal farther than he had gone on the former day. Presently he saw a civet cat, and, believing it to be the animal he was in search of, he killed it, bound it, and dragged it home, singing,

"Oh, mother, I have killed
The noondah, eater of the people."

When his mother saw the civet cat, she said, "My son, this is not the noondah, eater of the people." And he threw it away.

Again his mother entreated him to stay at home, but he would not listen to her, and started off again.

This time he went away off into the forest, and seeing a bigger cat than the last one, he killed it, bound it, and dragged it home, singing,

"Oh, mother, I have killed
The noondah, eater of the people."

But directly his mother saw it, she had to tell him, as before, "My son, this is not the noondah, eater of the people."

He was, of course, very much troubled at this; and his mother said, "Now, where do you expect to find this noondah? You don't know where it is, and you don't know what it looks like. You'll get sick over this; you're not looking so well now as you did. Come, stay at home."

But he said: "There are three things, one of which I shall do: I shall die; I shall find the noondah and kill it; or I shall return home unsuccessful. In any case, I'm off again."

This time he went farther than before, saw a zebra, killed it, bound it, and dragged it home, singing,

"Oh, mother, I have killed
The noondah, eater of the people."

Of course his mother had to tell him, once again, "My son, this is not the noondah, eater of the people."

After a good deal of argument, in which his mother's persuasion, as usual, was of no avail, he went off again, going farther than ever, when he caught a giraffe; and when he had killed it he said: "Well, this time I've been successful. This must be the noondah." So he dragged it home, singing,

"Oh, mother, I have killed
The noondah, eater of the people."

Again his mother had to assure him, "My son, this is not the noondah, eater of the people." She then pointed out to him that his brothers were not running about hunting for the noondah, but staying at home attending to their own business. But, remarking that all brothers were not alike, he expressed his determination to stick to his task until it came to a successful termination, and went off again, a still greater distance than before.

While going through the wilderness he espied a rhinoceros asleep under a tree, and turning to his attendants he exclaimed, "At last I see the noondah."

"Where, master?" they all cried, eagerly.

"There, under the tree."

"Oh-h! What shall we do?" they asked.

And he answered: "First of all, let us eat our fill, then we will attack it. We have found it in a good place, though if it kills us, we can't help it."

So they all took out their arrowroot cakes and ate till they were satisfied.

Then Mkaaah Jeechonee said, "Each of you take two guns; lay one beside you and take the other in your hands, and at the proper time let us all fire at once."

And they said, "All right, master."

So they crept cautiously through the bushes and got around to the other side of the tree, at the back of the rhinoceros; then they closed up till they were quite near it, and all fired together. The beast jumped up, ran a little way, and then fell down dead.

They bound it, and dragged it for two whole days, until they reached the town, when Mkaaah Jeechonee began singing,

"Oh, mother, I have killed
The noondah, eater of the people."

But he received the same answer from his mother: "My son, this is not the noondah, eater of the people."

And many persons came and looked at the rhinoceros, and felt very sorry for the young man. As for his father and mother, they both begged of him to give up, his father offering to give him anything he possessed if he would only stay at home. But he said, "I don't hear what you are saying; good-bye," and was off again.

This time he still further increased the distance from his home, and at last he saw an elephant asleep at noon in the forest. Thereupon he said to his attendants, "Now we have found the noondah."

"Ah, where is he?" said they.

"Yonder, in the shade. Do you see it?"

"Oh, yes, master; shall we march up to it?"

"If we march up to it, and it is looking this way, it will come at us, and if it does that, some of us will be killed. I think we had best let one man steal up close and see which way its face is turned."

As every one thought this was a good idea, a slave named Keerobo'to crept on his hands and knees, and had a good look at it. When he returned in the same manner, his master asked: "Well, what's the news? Is it the noondah?"

"I do not know," replied Keeroboto; "but I think there is very little doubt that it is. It is broad, with a very big head, and, goodness, I never saw such large ears!"

"All right," said Mkaaah Jeechonee; "let us eat, and then go for it."

So they took their arrowroot cakes, and their molasses cakes, and ate until they were quite full.

Then the youth said to them: "My people, to-day is perhaps the last we shall ever see; so we will take leave of each other. Those who are to escape will escape, and those who are to die will die; but if I die, let those who escape tell my mother and father not to grieve for me."

But his attendants said, "Oh, come along, master; none of us will die, please God."

So they went on their hands and knees till they were close up, and then they said to Mkaaah Jeechonee, "Give us your plan, master;" but he said, "There is no plan, only let all fire at once."

Well, they fired all at once, and immediately the elephant jumped up and charged at them. Then such a helter-skelter flight as there was! They threw away their guns and everything they carried, and made for the trees, which they climbed with surprising alacrity.

As to the elephant, he kept straight ahead until he fell down some distance away.

They all remained in the trees from three until six o'clock in the morning, without food and without clothing.

The young man sat in his tree and wept bitterly, saying, "I don't exactly know what death is, but it seems to me this must be very like it." As no one could see any one else, he did not know where his attendants were, and though he wished to come down from the tree, he thought, "Maybe the noondah is down below there, and will eat me."

Each attendant was in exactly the same fix, wishing to come down, but afraid the noondah was waiting to eat him.

Keeroboto had seen the elephant fall, but was afraid to get down by himself, saying, "Perhaps, though it has fallen down, it is not dead." But presently he saw a dog go up to it and smell it, and then he was sure it was dead. Then he got down from the tree as fast as he could and gave a signal cry, which was answered; but not being sure from whence the answer came, he repeated the cry, listening intently. When it was answered he went straight to the place from which the sound proceeded, and found two of his companions in one tree. To them he said, "Come on; get down; the noondah is dead." So they got down quickly and hunted around until they found their master. When they told him the news, he came down also; and after a little the attendants had all gathered together and had picked up their guns and their clothes, and were all right again. But they were all weak and hungry, so they rested and ate some food, after which they went to examine their prize.

As soon as Mkaaah Jeechonee saw it he said, "Ah, this is the noondah! This is it! This is it!" And they all agreed that it was it.

So they dragged the elephant three days to their town, and then the youth began singing,

"Oh, mother, this is he,

The noondah, eater of the people."

He was, naturally, quite upset when his mother replied, "My son, this is not the noondah, eater of the people." She further said: "Poor boy! what trouble you have been through. All the people are astonished that one so young should have such a great understanding!"

Then his father and mother began their entreaties again, and finally it was agreed that this next trip should be his last, whatever the result might be.

Well, they started off again, and went on and on, past the forest, until they came to a very high mountain, at the foot of which they camped for the night.

In the morning they cooked their rice and ate it, and then Mkaaah Jeechonee said: "Let us now climb the mountain, and look all over the country from its peak." And they went and they went, until after a long, weary while, they reached the top, where they sat down to rest and form their plans.

Now, one of the attendants, named Shindaa'no, while walking about, cast his eyes down the side of the mountain, and suddenly saw a great beast about half way down; but he could not make out its appearance distinctly, on account of the distance and the trees. Calling his master, he pointed it out to him, and something in Mkaaah Jeechonee's heart told him that it was the noondah. To make sure, however, he took his gun and his spear and went partly down the mountain to get a better view.

"Ah," said he, "this must be the noondah. My mother told me its ears were small, and those are small; she told me the noondah is broad and short, and so is this; she said it has two blotches, like a civet cat, and there are the blotches; she told me the tail is thick, and there is a thick tail. It must be the noondah."

Then he went back to his attendants and bade them eat heartily, which they did. Next he told them to leave every unnecessary thing behind, because if they had to run they would be better without encumbrance, and if they were victorious they could return for their goods.

When they had made all their arrangements they started down the mountain, but when they had got about half way down Keeroboto and Shindaano were afraid. Then the youth said to them: "Oh, let's go on; don't be afraid. We all have to live and die. What are you frightened about?" So, thus encouraged, they went on.

When they came near the place, Mkaaah Jeechonee ordered them to take off all their clothing except one piece, and to place that tightly on their bodies, so that if they had to run they would not be caught by thorns or branches.

So when they came close to the beast, they saw that it was asleep, and all agreed that it was the noondah.

Then the young man said, "Now the sun is setting, shall we fire at it, or let be till morning?"

And they all wished to fire at once, and see what the result would be without further tax on their nerves; therefore they arranged that they should all fire together.

They all crept up close, and when the master gave the word, they discharged their guns together. The noondah did not move; that one dose had been sufficient. Nevertheless, they all turned and scampered up to the top of the mountain. There they ate and rested for the night.

In the morning they ate their rice, and then went down to see how matters were, when they found the beast lying dead.

After resting and eating, they started homeward, dragging the dead beast with them. On the fourth day it began to give indications of decay, and the attendants wished to abandon it; but Mkaaah Jeechonee said they would continue to drag it if there was only one bone left.

When they came near the town he began to sing,

"Mother, mother, I have come
From the evil spirits, home.
Mother, listen while I sing;
While I tell you what I bring.
Oh, mother, I have killed
The noondah, eater of the people."

And when his mother looked out, she cried, "My son, this is the noondah, eater of the people."

Then all the people came out to welcome him, and his father was overcome with joy, and loaded him with honors, and procured him a rich and beautiful wife; and when he died Mkaaah Jeechonee became sultan, and lived long and happily, beloved by all the people.

JUSTICE

SIFIRWAKANGE and KASOKAMBIRYE

☾

Uganda (Baganda)

It happened once upon a time that a man Sifirwakange (I will not lose mine), who lived in Singo and who had two cows, had two visitors come to him to ask him to assist them and lend them some money, because they were in debt; he lent them the amount they required, and they went off saying to one another, "He will never find us again." As the men did not return, Sifirwakange set out and hunted all Uganda to discover them, and at last he found them. They were surprised and said: "We thought that by coming here you would never find us again, and we said we would never refund the money. However, here it is, take it."

When they had refunded the money and Sifirwakange had gone, they told Kasokambirye (Since I ate them) of Kyagwe about the money. They said, "That man will never lose his money." Kasokambirye said, "Let me go and borrow from him, and return home and see if he can find me." He therefore set out and went to Singo to Sifirwakange, and greeted him. Sifirwakange called his wife and told her to cook a meal for the stranger. Kasokambirye said, "My friend, I do not know you, but when I heard of your kindness I determined to find you, and have come because I am in debt and it is pressing heavily upon me; I beg you will give me a cow, and I will repay you later on when I can obtain one." Sifirwakange said "I cannot refuse to lend it to you, therefore take the cow and pay your debt." Kasokambirye thanked him and set off home to his wife; when he arrived he told her he had borrowed the cow from Sifirwakange, and added, "He does not know where our house is." He therefore proposed to kill and eat the cow.

At the end of five months Sifirwakange said to his wife: "I want to go to Kasokambirye and ask him to repay his debt." His wife asked him: "Do you know where he lives?" He replied: "Even though I do not know I will find him." Sifirwakange set out, and went to Kyagwe and found Kasokambirye sitting in the shade of his doorway; when he saw Sifirwakange he slipped away into a bundle of firewood. Sifirwakange pretended he had not seen Kasokambirye, and asked the man's wife, "Where is your husband?" She said, "He went away a long time ago and I do not know where he has gone." Sifirwakange said, "Let me take this bundle of firewood and go and make a fire, because I have no firewood." As he took it up Kasokambirye came out. Sifirwakange said, "My friend, is this the way you behave when you are sought for debt? You turn into a bundle of firewood." Kasokambirye said, "I live in firewood." Sifirwakange said, "I have come for my cow." Kasokambirye said, "Do not be angry about it, I will restore it in two days."

Sifirwakange returned to the place where he was staying, and waited two days and then returned. When he was nearing the house he saw Kasokambirye eating his food. When the latter saw Sifirwakange coming, he entered into the plantain food; Sifirwakange drew near and asked Kasokambirye's wife where her husband was, she replied, "He has gone to look for your cow." Sifirwakange said, "He told me to come to-day and promised to give it to me, and you say he has gone away." The woman replied, "Come again in the morning and see him." Sifirwakange agreed to do so, but said, "Give me some food." The woman offered him some, which he refused and said, "I want that basket of food which is near you." The woman had no excuse for refusing it, and he took it away. As he was about to eat it Kasokambirye called out, "Don't eat me," to which Sifirwakange answered, "Your wife told me you had gone away, and here you have hidden in the food." Kasokambirye laughed and said, "There is no deceiving you; remain here and my wife will bring the cow." The woman was sent and brought the cow and gave it to Sifirwakange, who also laughed and said, "You thought you were going to be too sharp for me and escape by your magical skill." Kasokambirye told his wife to cook a meal which they ate together and Sifirwakange returned home. When he arrived he said to his wife, "I have come with my cow," to which she answered, "I congratulate you upon your return, and also in bringing back the cow, which I did not expect you would find."

HAAMDAANEE

Tanzania

Once there was a very poor man, named Haamdaa'nee, who begged from door to door for his living, sometimes taking things before they were offered him. After a while people became suspicious of him, and stopped giving him anything, in order to keep him away from their houses. So at last he was reduced to the necessity of going every morning to the village dust heap, and picking up and eating the few grains of the tiny little millet seed that he might find there.

One day, as he was scratching and turning over the heap, he found a dime, which he tied up in a corner of his ragged dress, and continued to hunt for millet grains, but could not find one.

"Oh, well," said he, "I've got a dime now; I'm pretty well fixed. I'll go home and take a nap instead of a meal."

So he went to his hut, took a drink of water, put some tobacco in his mouth, and went to sleep.

The next morning, as he scratched in the dust heap, he saw a countryman going along, carrying a basket made of twigs, and he called to him: "Hi, there, country-man! What have you in that cage?"

The countryman, whose name was Moohaad'eem, replied, "Gazelles."

And Haamdaanee called: "Bring them here. Let me see them."

Now there were three well-to-do men standing near; and when they saw the countryman coming to Haamdaanee they smiled, and said, "You're taking lots of trouble for nothing, Moohaadeem."

"How's that, gentlemen?" he inquired.

"Why," said they, "that poor fellow has nothing at all. Not a cent."

"Oh, I don't know that," said the countryman; "he may have plenty, for all I know."

"Not he," said they.

"Don't you see for yourself," continued one of them, "that he is on the dust heap? Every day he scratches there like a hen, trying to get enough grains of millet to keep himself alive. If he had any money, wouldn't he buy a square meal, for once in his life? Do you think he would want to buy a gazelle? What would he do with it? He can't find enough food for himself, without looking for any for a gazelle."

But Moohaad'eem said: "Gentlemen, I have brought some goods here to sell. I answer all who call me, and if any one says 'Come,' I go to him. I don't favor one and slight another; therefore, as this man called me, I'm going to him."

"All right," said the first man; "you don't believe us. Well, we know where he lives, and all about him, and we know that he can't buy anything."

"That's so," said the second man. "Perhaps, however, you will see that we were right, after you have a talk with him."

To which the third man added, "Clouds are a sign of rain, but we have seen no signs of his being about to spend any money."

"All right, gentlemen," said Moohaadeem; "many better-looking people than he call me, and when I show them my gazelles they say, 'Oh, yes, they're very beautiful, but awfully dear; take them away.' So I shall not be disappointed if this man says the same thing. I shall go to him, anyhow."

Then one of the three men said, "Let us go with this man, and see what the beggar will buy."

"Pshaw!" said another; "buy! You talk foolishly. He has not had a good meal in three years, to my knowledge; and a man in his condition doesn't have money to buy gazelles. However, let's go; and if he makes this poor countryman carry his load over there just for the fun of looking at the gazelles, let each of us give him a good hard whack with our walking-sticks, to teach him how to behave toward honest merchants."

So, when they came near him, one of those three men said: "Well, here are the gazelles; now buy one. Here they are, you old hypocrite; you'll feast your eyes on them, but you can't buy them."

But Haamdaanee, paying no attention to the men, said to Moohaadeem, "How much for one of your gazelles?"

Then another of those men broke in: "You're very innocent, aren't you? You know, as well as I do, that gazelles are sold every day at two for a quarter."

Still taking no notice of these outsiders, Haamdaanee continued, "I'd like to buy one for a dime."

"One for a dime!" laughed the men; "of course you'd like to buy one for a dime. Perhaps you'd also like to have the dime to buy with."

Then one of them gave him a push on the cheek.

At this Haamdaanee turned and said: "Why do you push me on the cheek, when I've done nothing to you? I do not know you. I call this man, to transact some business with him, and you, who are strangers, step in to spoil our trade."

He then untied the knot in the corner of his ragged coat, produced the dime, and, handing it to Moohaadeem, said, "Please, good man, let me have a gazelle for that."

At this, the countryman took a small gazelle out of the cage and handed it to him, saying, "Here, master, take this one. I call it Keejee'paa." Then turning to those three men, he laughed, and said: "Ehe! How's this? You, with your white robes, and turbans, and swords, and daggers, and sandals on your feet— you gentlemen of property, and no mistake—you told me this man was too poor to buy anything; yet he has bought a gazelle for a dime, while you fine fellows, I think, haven't enough money among you to buy half a gazelle, if they were five cents each."

Then Moohaadeem and the three men went their several ways.

As for Haamdaanee, he stayed at the dust heap until he found a few grains of millet for himself and a few for Keejeepaa, the gazelle, and then went to his hut, spread his sleeping mat, and he and the gazelle slept together.

This going to the dust heap for a few grains of millet and then going home to bed continued for about a week.

Then one night Haamdaanee was awakened by some one calling, "Master!" Sitting up, he answered: "Here I am. Who calls?" The gazelle answered, "I do!"

Upon this, the beggar man became so scared that he did not know whether he should faint or get up and run away.

Seeing him so overcome, Keejeepaa asked, "Why, master, what's the matter?"

"Oh, gracious!" he gasped; "what a wonder I see!"

"A wonder?" said the gazelle, looking all around; "why, what is this wonder, that makes you act as if you were all broken up?"

"Why, it's so wonderful, I can hardly believe I'm awake!" said his master. "Who in the world ever before knew of a gazelle that could speak?"

"Oho!" laughed Keejeepaa; "is that all? There are many more wonderful things than that. But now, listen, while I tell you why I called you."

"Certainly; I'll listen to every word," said the man. "I can't help listening!"

"Well, you see, it's just this way," said Keejeepaa; "I've allowed you to become my master, and I can not run away from you; so I want you to make an agreement with me, and I will make you a promise, and keep it."

"Say on," said his master.

"Now," continued the gazelle, "one doesn't have to be acquainted with you long, in order to discover that you are very poor. This scratching a few grains of millet from the dust heap every day, and managing to subsist upon them, is all very well for you—you're used to it, because it's a matter of necessity with you; but if I keep it up much longer, you won't have any gazelle—Keejeepaa will die of starvation. Therefore, I want to go away every day and feed on my own kind of food; and I promise you I will return every evening."

"Well, I guess I'll have to give my consent," said the man, in no very cheerful tone.

As it was now dawn, Keejeepaa jumped up and ran out of the door, Haamdaanee following him. The gazelle ran very fast, and his master stood watching him until he disappeared. Then tears started in the man's eyes, and, raising his hands, he cried, "Oh, my mother!" Then he cried, "Oh, my father!" Then he cried, "Oh, my gazelle! It has run away!"

Some of his neighbors, who heard him carrying on in this manner, took the opportunity to inform him that he was a fool, an idiot, and a dissipated fellow.

Said one of them: "You hung around that dust heap, goodness knows how long, scratching like a hen, till fortune gave you a dime. You hadn't sense enough to go and buy some decent food; you had to buy a gazelle. Now you've let the creature run away. What are you crying about? You brought all your trouble on yourself."

All this, of course, was very comforting to Haamdaanee, who slunk off to the dust heap, got a few grains of millet, and came back to his hut, which now seemed meaner and more desolate than ever.

At sunset, however, Keejeepaa came trotting in; and the beggar was happy again, and said, "Ah, my friend, you have returned to me."

"Of course," said the gazelle; "didn't I promise you? You see, I feel that when you bought me you gave all the money you had in the world, even though it was only a dime. Why, then, should I grieve you? I couldn't do it. If I go and get myself some food, I'll always come back evenings."

When the neighbors saw the gazelle come home every evening and run off every morning, they were greatly surprised, and began to suspect that Haamdaanee was a wizard.

Well, this coming and going continued for five days, the gazelle telling its master each night what fine places it had been to, and what lots of food it had eaten.

On the sixth day it was feeding among some thorn bushes in a thick wood, when, scratching away some bitter grass at the foot of a big tree, it saw an immense diamond of intense brightness.

"Oho!" said Keejeepaa, in great astonishment; "here's property, and no mistake! This is worth a kingdom! If I take it to my master he will be killed; for, being a poor man, if they say to him, 'Where did you get it?' and he answers, 'I picked it up,' they will not believe him; if he says, 'It was given to me,' they will not believe him either. It will not do for me to get my master into difficulties. I know what I'll do. I'll seek some powerful person; he will use it properly."

So Keejeepaa started off through the forest, holding the diamond in his mouth, and ran, and ran, but saw no town that day; so he slept in the forest, and arose at dawn and pursued his way. And the second day passed like the first.

On the third day the gazelle had traveled from dawn until between eight and nine o'clock, when he began to see scattered houses, getting larger in size, and

HAAMDAANEE

❋ 81 ❋

knew he was approaching a town. In due time he found himself in the main street of a large city, leading direct to the sultan's palace, and began to run as fast as he could. People passing along stopped to look at the strange sight of a gazelle running swiftly along the main street with something wrapped in green leaves between its teeth.

The sultan was sitting at the door of his palace, when Keejeepaa, stopping a little way off, dropped the diamond from its mouth, and, lying down beside it, panting, called out: "Ho, there! Ho, there!" which is a cry every one makes in that part of the world when wishing to enter a house, remaining outside until the cry is answered.

After the cry had been repeated several times, the sultan said to his attendants, "Who is doing all that calling?"

And one answered, "Master, it's a gazelle that's calling, 'Ho, there!'"

"Ho-ho!" said the sultan; "Ho-ho! Invite the gazelle to come near."

Then three attendants ran to Keejeepaa and said: "Come, get up. The sultan commands you to come near."

So the gazelle arose, picked up the diamond, and, approaching the sultan, laid the jewel at his feet, saying, "Master, good afternoon!" To which the sultan replied: "May God make it good! Come near."

The sultan ordered his attendants to bring a carpet and a large cushion, and desired the gazelle to rest upon them. When it protested that it was comfortable as it was, he insisted, and Keejeepaa had to allow himself to be made a very honored guest. Then they brought milk and rice, and the sultan would hear nothing until the gazelle had fed and rested.

At last, when everything had been disposed of, the sultan said, "Well, now, my friend, tell me what news you bring."

And Keejeepaa said: "Master, I don't exactly know how you will like the news I bring. The fact is, I'm sent here to insult you! I've come to try and pick a quarrel with you! In fact, I'm here to propose a family alliance with you!"

At this the sultan exclaimed: "Oh, come! for a gazelle, you certainly know how to talk! Now, the fact of it is, I'm looking for some one to insult me. I'm just aching to have some one pick a quarrel with me. I'm impatient for a family alliance. Go on with your message."

Then Keejeepaa said, "You don't bear any ill will against me, who am only a messenger?"

And the sultan said, "None at all."

"Well," said Keejeepaa, "look at this pledge I bring;" dropping the diamond wrapped in leaves into the sultan's lap.

When the sultan opened the leaves and saw the great, sparkling jewel, he was overcome with astonishment. At last he said, "Well?"

"I have brought this pledge," said the gazelle, "from my master, Sultan Daaraa'ee. He has heard that you have a daughter, so he sent you this jewel, hoping you will forgive him for not sending something more worthy of your acceptance than this trifle."

"Goodness!" said the sultan to himself; "he calls this a trifle!" Then to the gazelle: "Oh, that's all right; that's all right. I'm satisfied. The Sultan Daaraaee has my consent to marry my daughter, and I don't want a single thing from him. Let him come empty-handed. If he has more of these trifles, let him leave them at home. This is my message, and I hope you will make it perfectly clear to your master."

The gazelle assured him that he would explain everything satisfactorily, adding: "And now, master, I take my leave. I go straight to our own town, and hope that in about eleven days we shall return to be your guests." So, with mutual compliments, they parted.

In the meantime, Haamdaanee was having an exceedingly tough time. Keejeepaa having disappeared, he wandered about the town moaning, "Oh, my poor gazelle! my poor gazelle!" while the neighbors laughed and jeered at him, until, between them and his loss, he was nearly out of his mind.

But one evening, when he had gone to bed, Keejeepaa walked in. Up he jumped, and began to embrace the gazelle, and weep over it, and carry on at a great rate.

When he thought there had been about enough of this kind of thing, the gazelle said: "Come, come; keep quiet, my master. I've brought you good news." But the beggar man continued to cry and fondle, and declare that he had thought his gazelle was dead.

At last Keejeepaa said: "Oh, well, master, you see I'm all right. You must brace up, and prepare to hear my news, and do as I advise you."

"Go on; go on," replied his master; "explain what you will, I'll do whatever you require me to do. If you were to say, 'Lie down on your back, that I may roll you over the side of the hill,' I would lie down."

"Well," said the gazelle, "there is not much to explain just now, but I'll tell you this: I've seen many kinds of food, food that is desirable and food that is objectionable, but this food I'm about to offer you is very sweet indeed."

"What?" said Haamdaanee. "Is it possible that in this world there is anything that is positively good? There must be good and bad in everything. Food that is both sweet and bitter is good food, but if food were nothing but sweetness would it not be injurious?"

"H'm!" yawned the gazelle; "I'm too tired to talk philosophy. Let's go to sleep now, and when I call you in the morning, all you have to do is to get up and follow me."

So at dawn they set forth, the gazelle leading the way, and for five days they journeyed through the forest.

On the fifth day they came to a stream, and Keejeepaa said to his master, "Lie down here." When he had done so, the gazelle set to and beat him so soundly that he cried out: "Oh, let up, I beg of you!"

"Now," said the gazelle, "I'm going away, and when I return I expect to find you right here; so don't you leave this spot on any account." Then he ran away, and about ten o'clock that morning he arrived at the house of the sultan.

Now, ever since the day Keejeepaa left the town, soldiers had been placed along the road to watch for and announce the approach of Sultan Daaraaee; so one of them, when he saw the gazelle in the distance, rushed up and cried to the sultan, "Sultan Daaraaee is coming! I've seen the gazelle running as fast as it can in this direction."

The sultan and his attendants immediately set out to meet his guests; but when they had gone a little way beyond the town they met the gazelle coming along alone, who, on reaching the sultan, said, "Good day, my master." The sultan replied in kind, and asked the news, but Keejeepaa said: "Ah, do not ask me. I can scarcely walk, and my news is bad!"

"Why, how is that?" asked the sultan.

"Oh, dear!" sighed the gazelle; "such misfortune and misery! You see, Sultan Daaraaee and I started alone to come here, and we got along all right until we came to the thick part of the forest yonder, when we were met by robbers, who seized my master, bound him, beat him, and took everything he had, even stripping off every stitch of his clothing. Oh, dear! oh, dear!"

"Dear me!" said the sultan; "we must attend to this at once." So, hurrying back with his attendants to his house, he called a groom, to whom he said, "Saddle the best horse in my stable, and put on him my finest harness." Then he directed a woman servant to open the big inlaid chest and bring him a bag of clothes. When she brought it he picked out a loin-cloth, and a long white robe, and a black over-jacket, and a shawl for the waist, and a turban cloth, all of the very finest. Then he sent for a curved sword with a gold hilt, and a curved dagger with gold filigree, and a pair of elegant sandals, and a fine walking-cane.

Then the sultan said to Keejeepaa, "Take some of my soldiers, and let them convey these things to Sultan Daaraaee, that he may dress himself and come to me."

But the gazelle answered: "Ah, my master, can I take these soldiers with me and put Sultan Daaraaee to shame? There he lies, beaten and robbed, and I would not have any one see him. I can take everything by myself."

"Why," exclaimed the sultan, "here is a horse, and there are clothes and arms. I don't see how a little gazelle can manage all those things."

But the gazelle had them fasten everything on the horse's back, and tie the end of the bridle around his own neck, and then he set off alone, amidst the wonder and admiration of the people of that city, high and low.

When he arrived at the place where he had left the beggar-man, he found him lying waiting for him, and overjoyed at his return.

"Now," said he, "I have brought you the sweet food I promised. Come, get up and bathe yourself."

With the hesitation of a person long unaccustomed to such a thing, the man stepped into the stream and began to wet himself a little.

"Oh," said the gazelle, impatiently, "a little water like that won't do you much good; get out into the deep pool."

"Dear me!" said the man, timidly; "there is so much water there; and where there is much water there are sure to be horrible animals."

"Animals! What kind of animals?"

"Well, crocodiles, water lizards, snakes, and, at any rate, frogs; and they bite people, and I'm terribly afraid of all of them."

"Oh, well," said Keejeepaa, "do the best you can in the stream; but rub yourself well with earth, and, for goodness' sake, scrub your teeth well with sand; they are awfully dirty."

So the man obeyed, and soon made quite a change in his appearance.

Then the gazelle said: "Here, hurry up and put on these things. The sun has gone down, and we ought to have started before this."

So the man dressed himself in the fine clothes the sultan had sent, and then he mounted the horse, and they started; the gazelle trotting on ahead.

When they had gone some distance, the gazelle stopped, and said, "See here: nobody who sees you now would suspect that you are the man who scratched in the dust heap yesterday. Even if we were to go back to our town the neighbors would not recognize you, if it were only for the fact that your face is clean and your teeth are white. Your appearance is all right, but I have a caution to give you. Over there, where we are going, I have procured for you the sultan's daughter for a wife, with all the usual wedding gifts. Now, you must keep quiet. Say nothing except, 'How d'ye do?' and 'What's the news?' Let me do the talking."

"All right," said the man; "that suits me exactly."

"Do you know what your name is?"

"Of course I do."

"Indeed? Well, what is it?"

"Why, my name is Haamdaanee."

"Not much," laughed Keejeepaa; "your name is Sultan Daaraaee."

"Oh, is it?" said his master. "That's good."

So they started forward again, and in a little while they saw soldiers running in every direction, and fourteen of these joined them to escort them. Then they saw ahead of them the sultan, and the viziers, and the emirs, and the judges, and the great men of the city, coming to meet them.

"Now, then," said Keejeepaa, "get off your horse and salute your father-in-law. That's him in the middle, wearing the sky-blue jacket."

"All right," said the man, jumping off his horse, which was then led by a soldier.

So the two met, and the sultans shook hands, and kissed each other, and walked up to the palace together.

Then they had a great feast, and made merry and talked until night, at which time Sultan Daaraaee and the gazelle were put into an inner room, with three soldiers at the door to guard and attend upon them.

When the morning came, Keejeepaa went to the sultan and said: "Master, we wish to attend to the business which brought us here. We want to marry your daughter, and the sooner the ceremony takes place, the better it will please the Sultan Daaraaee."

"Why, that's all right," said the sultan; "the bride is ready. Let some one call the teacher, Mwaaleemoo, and tell him to come at once."

When Mwaaleemoo arrived, the sultan said, "See here, we want you to marry this gentleman to my daughter right away."

"All right; I'm ready," said the teacher. So they were married.

Early the next morning the gazelle said to his master: "Now I'm off on a journey. I shall be gone about a week; but however long I am gone, don't you leave the house till I return. Good-bye."

Then he went to the real sultan and said: "Good master, Sultan Daaraaee has ordered me to return to our town and put his house in order; he commands me to be here again in a week; if I do not return by that time, he will stay here until I come."

The sultan asked him if he would not like to have some soldiers go with him; but the gazelle replied that he was quite competent to take care of himself, as his previous journeys had proved, and he preferred to go alone; so with mutual good wishes they parted.

But Keejeepaa did not go in the direction of the old village. He struck off by another road through the forest, and after a time came to a very fine town, of large, handsome houses. As he went through the principal street, right to the far end, he was greatly astonished to observe that the town seemed to have no inhabitants, for he saw neither man, woman, nor child in all the place.

At the end of the main street he came upon the largest and most beautiful house he had ever seen, built of sapphire, and turquoise, and costly marbles.

"Oh, my!" said the gazelle; "this house would just suit my master. I'll have to pluck up my courage and see whether this is deserted like the other houses in this mysterious town."

So Keejeepaa knocked at the door, and called, "Hullo, there!" several times; but no one answered. And he said to himself: "This is strange! If there were no one inside, the door would be fastened on the outside. Perhaps they are in another part of the house, or asleep. I'll call again, louder."

So he called again, very loud and long, "Hul-lo, th-e-re! Hul-lo!" And directly an old woman inside answered, "Who is that calling so loudly?"

"It is I, your grandchild, good mistress," said Keejeepaa.

"If you are my grandchild," replied the old woman, "go back to your home at once; don't come and die here, and bring me to my death also."

"Oh, come," said he, "open the door, mistress; I have just a few words I wish to say to you."

"My dear grandson," she replied, "the only reason why I do not open the door is because I fear to endanger both your life and my own."

"Oh, don't worry about that; I guess your life and mine are safe enough for a while. Open the door, anyhow, and hear the little I have to say."

So the old woman opened the door.

Then they exchanged salutations and compliments, after which she asked the gazelle, "What's the news from your place, grandson?"

"Oh, everything is going along pretty well," said he; "what's the news around here?"

"Ah!" sighed the old creature; "the news here is very bad. If you're looking for a place to die in, you've struck it here. I've not the slightest doubt you'll see all you want of death this very day."

"Huh!" replied Keejeepaa, lightly; "for a fly to die in honey is not bad for the fly, and doesn't injure the honey."

"It may be all very well for you to be easy about it," persisted the old person; "but if people with swords and shields did not escape, how can a little thing like you avoid danger? I must again beg of you to go back to the place you came from. Your safety seems of more interest to me than it is to you."

"Well, you see, I can't go back just now; and besides, I want to find out more about this place. Who owns it?"

"Ah, grandson, in this house are enormous wealth, numbers of people, hundreds of horses, and the owner is Neeo'ka Mkoo', the wonderfully big snake. He owns this whole town, also."

"Oho! Is that so?" said Keejeepaa. "Look here, old lady; can't you put me on to some plan of getting near this big snake, that I may kill him?"

"Mercy!" cried the old woman, in affright; "don't talk like that. You've put my life in danger already, for I'm sure Neeoka Mkoo can hear what is said in this house, wherever he is. You see I'm a poor old woman, and I have been placed here, with those pots and pans, to cook for him. Well, when the big snake is coming, the wind begins to blow and the dust flies as it would do in a great storm. Then, when he arrives in the courtyard, he eats until he is full, and after that, goes inside there to drink water. When he has finished, he goes away again. This occurs every other day, just when the sun is overhead. I may add that Neeoka Mkoo has seven heads. Now, then, do you think yourself a match for him?"

"Look here, mother," said the gazelle, "don't you worry about me. Has this big snake a sword?"

"He has. This is it," said she, taking from its peg a very keen and beautiful blade, and handing it to him; "but what's the use in bothering about it? We are dead already."

"We shall see about that," said Keejeepaa.

Just at that moment the wind began to blow, and the dust to fly, as if a great storm were approaching.

"Do you hear the great one coming?" cried the old woman.

"Pshaw!" said the gazelle; "I'm a great one also—and I have the advantage of being on the inside. Two bulls can't live in one cattle-pen. Either he will live in this house, or I will."

Notwithstanding the terror the old lady was in, she had to smile at the assurance of this little undersized gazelle, and repeated over again her account of the people with swords and shields who had been killed by the big snake.

"Ah, stop your gabbling!" said the gazelle; "you can't always judge a banana by its color or size. Wait and see, grandma."

In a very little while the big snake, Neeoka Mkoo, came into the courtyard, and went around to all the pots and ate their contents. Then he came to the door.

"Hullo, old lady," said he; "how is it I smell a new kind of odor inside there?"

"Oh, that's nothing, good master," replied the old woman; "I've been so busy around here lately I haven't had time to look after myself; but this morning I used some perfume, and that's what you smell."

Now, Keejeepaa had drawn the sword, and was standing just inside the doorway; so, when the big snake put his head in, it was cut off so quickly that its owner did not know it was gone. When he put in his second head it was cut off with the same quickness; and, feeling a little irritation, he exclaimed, "Who's inside there, scratching me?" He then thrust in his third head, and that was cut off also.

This continued until six heads had been disposed of, when Neeoka Mkoo unfolded his rings and lashed around so that the gazelle and the old woman could not see one another through the dust.

Then the snake thrust in his seventh head, and the gazelle, crying: "Now your time has come; you've climbed many trees, but this you can not climb," severed it, and immediately fell down in a fainting fit.

Well, that old woman, although she was seventy-five years of age, jumped, and shouted, and laughed, like a girl of nine. Then she ran and got water, and sprinkled the gazelle, and turned him this way and that way, until at last he sneezed; which greatly pleased the old person, who fanned him and tended him until he was quite recovered.

"Oh, my!" said she; "who would have thought you could be a match for him, my grandson?"

"Well, well," said Keejeepaa; "that's all over. Now show me everything around this place."

So she showed him everything, from top to bottom: store-rooms full of goods, chambers full of expensive foods, rooms containing handsome people who had been kept prisoners for a long time, slaves, and everything.

Next he asked her if there was any person who was likely to lay claim to the place or make any trouble; and she answered: "No one; everything here belongs to you."

"Very well, then," said he, "you stay here and take care of these things until I bring my master. This place belongs to him now."

Keejeepaa stayed three days examining the house, and said to himself: "Well, when my master comes here he will be much pleased with what I have done for him, and he'll appreciate it after the life he's been accustomed to. As to his father-in-law, there is not a house in his town that can compare with this."

On the fourth day he departed, and in due time arrived at the town where the sultan and his master lived. Then there were great rejoicings; the sultan being particularly pleased at his return, while his master felt as if he had received a new lease of life.

After everything had settled down a little, Keejeepaa told his master he must be ready to go, with his wife, to his new home after four days. Then he went and told the sultan that Sultan Daaraaee desired to take his wife to his own town in four days; to which the sultan strongly objected; but the gazelle said it was his master's wish, and at last everything was arranged.

On the day of the departure a great company assembled to escort Sultan Daaraaee and his bride. There were the bride's ladies-in-waiting, and slaves, and horsemen, and Keejeepaa leading them all.

So they traveled three days, resting when the sun was overhead, and stopping each evening about five o'clock to eat and sleep; arising next morning at daybreak, eating, and going forward again. And all this time the gazelle took very little rest, going all through the company, from the ladies to the slaves, and seeing that every one was well supplied with food and quite comfortable; therefore the entire company loved him and valued him like the apples of their eyes.

On the fourth day, during the afternoon, many houses came into view, and some of the folks called Keejeepaa's attention to them. "Certainly," said he; "that is our town, and that house you see yonder is the palace of Sultan Daaraaee."

So they went on, and all the company filed into the courtyard, while the gazelle and his master went into the house.

When the old woman saw Keejeepaa, she began to dance, and shout, and carry on, just as she did when he killed Neeoka Mkoo, and taking up his foot she kissed it; but Keejeepaa said: "Old lady, let me alone; the one to be made much of is this my master, Sultan Daaraaee. Kiss his feet; he has the first honors whenever he is present."

The old woman excused herself for not knowing the master, and then Sultan Daaraaee and the gazelle went around on a tour of inspection. The sultan ordered all the prisoners to be released, the horses to be sent out to pasture, all the rooms to be swept, the furniture to be dusted, and, in the meantime, servants were busy preparing food. Then every one had apartments assigned to him, and all were satisfied.

After they had remained there some time, the ladies who had accompanied the bride expressed a desire to return to their own homes. Keejeepaa begged them not to hurry away, but after a while they departed, each loaded with gifts by the gazelle, for whom they had a thousand times more affection than for his master. Then things settled down to their regular routine.

One day the gazelle said to the old woman: "I think the conduct of my master is very singular. I have done nothing but good for him all the time I have been with him. I came to this town and braved many dangers for him, and when all was over I gave everything to him. Yet he has never asked: 'How did you get this house? How did you get this town? Who is the owner of this house? Have you rented all these things, or have they been given you? What has become of the inhabitants of the place?' I don't understand him. And further: although I have done nothing but good for him, he has never done one good thing for me. Nothing here is really his. He never saw such a house or town as this since the day he was born, and he doesn't own anything of it. I believe the old folks were right when they said, 'If you want to do any person good, don't do too much; do him a little harm occasionally, and he'll think more of you.' However, I've done all I can now, and I'd like to see him make some little return."

Next morning the old woman was awakened early by the gazelle calling, "Mother! Mother!" When she went to him she found he was sick in his stomach, feverish, and all his legs ached.

"Go," said he, "and tell my master I am very ill."

So she went upstairs and found the master and mistress sitting on a marble couch, covered with a striped silk scarf from India.

"Well," said the master, "what do you want, old woman?"

"Oh, my master," cried she, "Keejeepaa is sick!"

The mistress started and said: "Dear me! What is the matter with him?"

"All his body pains him. He is sick all over."

"Oh, well," said the master, "what can I do? Go and get some of that red millet, that is too common for our use, and make him some gruel."

"Gracious!" exclaimed his wife, staring at him in amazement; "do you wish her to feed our friend with stuff that a horse would not eat if he were ever so hungry? This is not right of you."

"Ah, get out!" said he, "you're crazy. We eat rice; isn't red millet good enough for a gazelle that cost only a dime?"

"Oh, but he is no ordinary gazelle. He should be as dear to you as the apple of your eye. If sand got in your eye it would trouble you."

"You talk too much," returned her husband; then, turning to the old woman, he said, "Go and do as I told you."

So the old woman went downstairs, and when she saw the gazelle, she began to cry, and say, "Oh, dear! oh, dear!"

It was a long while before the gazelle could persuade her to tell him what had passed upstairs, but at last she told him all. When he had heard it, he said: "Did he really tell you to make me red millet gruel?"

"Ah," cried she, "do you think I would say such a thing if it were not so?"

"Well," said Keejeepaa, "I believe what the old folks said was right. However, we'll give him another chance. Go up to him again, and tell him I am very sick, and that I can't eat that gruel."

So she went upstairs, and found the master and mistress sitting by the window, drinking coffee.

The master, looking around and seeing her, said: "What's the matter now, old woman?"

And she said: "Master, I am sent by Keejeepaa. He is very sick indeed, and has not taken the gruel you told me to make for him."

"Oh, bother!" he exclaimed. "Hold your tongue, and keep your feet still, and shut your eyes, and stop your ears with wax; then, if that gazelle tells you to come up here, say that your legs are stiff; and if he tells you to listen, say your ears are deaf; and if he tells you to look, say your sight has failed you; and if he wants you to talk, tell him your tongue is paralyzed."

When the old woman heard these words, she stood and stared, and was unable to move. As for his wife, her face became sad, and the tears began to start from her eyes; observing which, her husband said, sharply, "What's the matter with you, sultan's daughter?"

The lady replied, "A man's madness is his undoing."

"Why do you say that, mistress?" he inquired.

"Ah," said she, "I am grieved, my husband, at your treatment of Keejeepaa. Whenever I say a good word for the gazelle you dislike to hear it. I pity you that your understanding is gone."

"What do you mean by talking in that manner to me?" he blustered.

"Why, advice is a blessing, if properly taken. A husband should advise with his wife, and a wife with her husband; then they are both blessed."

"Oh, stop," said her husband, impatiently; "it's evident you've lost your senses. You should be chained up." Then he said to the old woman: "Never mind her talk; and as to this gazelle, tell him to stop bothering me and putting on style, as if he were the sultan. I can't eat, I can't drink, I can't sleep, because of that gazelle worrying me with his messages. First, the gazelle is sick; then, the gazelle doesn't like what he gets to eat. Confound it! If he likes to eat, let him eat; if he doesn't like to eat, let him die and be out of the way. My mother is dead, and my father is dead, and I still live and eat; shall I be put out of my way by a gazelle, that I bought for a dime, telling me he wants this thing or that thing? Go and tell him to learn how to behave himself toward his superiors."

When the old woman went downstairs, she found the gazelle was bleeding at the mouth, and in a very bad way. All she could say was, "My son, the good you did is all lost; but be patient."

And the gazelle wept with the old woman when she told him all that had passed, and he said, "Mother, I am dying, not only from sickness, but from shame and anger at this man's ingratitude."

After a while Keejeepaa told the old woman to go and tell the master that he believed he was dying. When she went upstairs she found Daaraaee chewing sugar-cane, and she said to him, "Master, the gazelle is worse; we think him nearer to dying than getting well."

To which he answered: "Haven't I told you often enough not to bother me?"

Then his wife said: "Oh, husband, won't you go down and see the poor gazelle? If you don't like to go, let me go and see him. He never gets a single good thing from you."

But he turned to the old woman and said, "Go and tell that nuisance of a gazelle to die eleven times if he chooses to."

"Now, husband," persisted the lady, "what has Keejeepaa done to you? Has he done you any wrong? Such words as yours people use to their enemies only. Surely the gazelle is not your enemy. All the people who know him, great and lowly, love him dearly, and they will think it very wrong of you if you neglect him. Now, do be kind to him, Sultan Daaraaee."

But he only repeated his assertion that she had lost her wits, and would have nothing further of argument.

So the old woman went down and found the gazelle worse than ever.

In the meantime Sultan Daaraaee's wife managed to give some rice to a servant to cook for the gazelle, and also sent him a soft shawl to cover him and a pillow to lie upon. She also sent him a message that if he wished, she would have her father's best physicians attend him.

All this was too late, however, for just as these good things arrived, Keejeepaa died.

When the people heard he was dead, they went running around crying and having an awful time; and when Sultan Daaraaee found out what all the commotion was about he was very indignant, remarking, "Why, you are making as much fuss as if I were dead, and all over a gazelle that I bought for a dime!"

But his wife said: "Husband, it was this gazelle that came to ask me of my father, it was he who brought me from my father's, and it was to him I was given by my father. He gave you everything good, and you do not possess a thing that he did not procure for you. He did everything he could to help you, and you not only returned him unkindness, but now he is dead you have ordered people to throw him into the well. Let us alone, that we may weep."

But the gazelle was taken and thrown into the well.

Then the lady wrote a letter telling her father to come to her directly, and despatched it by trusty messengers; upon the receipt of which the sultan and his attendants started hurriedly to visit his daughter.

When they arrived, and heard that the gazelle was dead and had been thrown into the well, they wept very much; and the sultan, and the vizier, and the judges, and the rich chief men, all went down into the well and brought up the body of Keejeepaa, and took it away with them and buried it.

Now, that night the lady dreamt that she was at home at her father's house; and when dawn came she awoke and found she was in her own bed in her own town again.

And her husband dreamed that he was on the dust heap, scratching; and when he awoke there he was, with both hands full of dust, looking for grains of millet. Staring wildly he looked around to the right and left, saying: "Oh, who has played this trick on me? How did I get back here, I wonder?"

Just then the children going along, and seeing him, laughed and hooted at him, calling out: "Hullo, Haamdaanee, where have you been? Where do you come from? We thought you were dead long ago."

So the sultan's daughter lived in happiness with her people until the end, and that beggar-man continued to scratch for grains of millet in the dust heap until he died.

If this story is good, the goodness belongs to all; if it is bad, the badness belongs only to him who told it.

THE APE, the SNAKE,
and the LION

Tanzania

Long, long ago there lived, in a village called Keejee'jee, a woman whose husband died, leaving her with a little baby boy. She worked hard all day to get food for herself and child, but they lived very poorly and were most of the time half-starved.

When the boy, whose name was 'Mvoo' Laa'na, began to get big, he said to his mother, one day: "Mother, we are always hungry. What work did my father do to support us?"

His mother replied: "Your father was a hunter. He set traps, and we ate what he caught in them."

"Oho!" said 'Mvoo Laana; "that's not work; that's fun. I, too, will set traps, and see if we can't get enough to eat."

The next day he went into the forest and cut branches from the trees, and returned home in the evening.

The second day he spent making the branches into traps.

The third day he twisted coconut fiber into ropes.

The fourth day he set up as many traps as time would permit.

The fifth day he set up the remainder of the traps.

The sixth day he went to examine the traps, and they had caught so much game, beside what they needed for themselves, that he took a great quantity to the big town of Oongoo'ja, where he sold it and bought corn and other things, and the house was full of food; and, as this good fortune continued, he and his mother lived very comfortably.

But after a while, when he went to his traps he found nothing in them day after day.

One morning, however, he found that an ape had been caught in one of the traps, and he was about to kill it, when it said: "Son of Adam, I am Neea'nee, the ape; do not kill me. Take me out of this trap and let me go. Save me from the rain, that I may come and save you from the sun some day."

So 'Mvoo Laana took him out of the trap and let him go.

When Neeanee had climbed up in a tree, he sat on a branch and said to the youth: "For your kindness I will give you a piece of advice: Believe me, men are all bad. Never do a good turn for a man; if you do, he will do you harm at the first opportunity."

The second day, 'Mvoo Laana found a snake in the same trap. He started to the village to give the alarm, but the snake shouted: "Come back, son of Adam; don't call the people from the village to come and kill me. I am Neeoka, the snake. Let me out of this trap, I pray you. Save me from the rain to-day, that I may be able to save you from the sun to-morrow, if you should be in need of help."

So the youth let him go; and as he went he said, "I will return your kindness if I can, but do not trust any man; if you do him a kindness he will do you an injury in return at the first opportunity."

The third day, 'Mvoo Laana found a lion in the same trap that had caught the ape and the snake, and he was afraid to go near it. But the lion said: "Don't run away; I am Sim'ba Kong'way, the very old lion. Let me out of this trap, and I will not hurt you. Save me from the rain, that I may save you from the sun if you should need help."

So 'Mvoo Laana believed him and let him out of the trap, and Simba Kongway, before going his way, said: "Son of Adam, you have been kind to me, and I will repay you with kindness if I can; but never do a kindness to a man, or he will pay you back with unkindness."

The next day a man was caught in the same trap, and when the youth released him, he repeatedly assured him that he would never forget the service he had done him in restoring his liberty and saving his life.

Well, it seemed that he had caught all the game that could be taken in traps, and 'Mvoo Laana and his mother were hungry every day, with nothing to satisfy

JUSTICE

them, as they had been before. At last he said to his mother, one day: "Mother, make me seven cakes of the little meal we have left, and I will go hunting with my bow and arrows." So she baked him the cakes, and he took them and his bow and arrows and went into the forest.

The youth walked and walked, but could see no game, and finally he found that he had lost his way, and had eaten all his cakes but one.

And he went on and on, not knowing whether he was going away from his home or toward it, until he came to the wildest and most desolate looking wood he had ever seen. He was so wretched and tired that he felt he must lie down and die, when suddenly he heard some one calling him, and looking up he saw Neeanee, the ape, who said, "Son of Adam, where are you going?"

"I don't know," replied 'Mvoo Laana, sadly; "I'm lost."

"Well, well," said the ape; "don't worry. Just sit down here and rest yourself until I come back, and I will repay with kindness the kindness you once showed me."

Then Neeanee went away off to some gardens and stole a whole lot of ripe pawpaws and bananas, and brought them to 'Mvoo Laana, and said: "Here's plenty of food for you. Is there anything else you want? Would you like a drink?" And before the youth could answer he ran off with a calabash and brought it back full of water. So the youth ate heartily, and drank all the water he needed, and then each said to the other, "Good-bye, till we meet again," and went their separate ways.

When 'Mvoo Laana had walked a great deal farther without finding which way he should go, he met Simba Kongway, who asked, "Where are you going, son of Adam?"

And the youth answered, as dolefully as before, "I don't know; I'm lost."

"Come, cheer up," said the very old lion, "and rest yourself here a little. I want to repay with kindness to-day the kindness you showed me on a former day."

So 'Mvoo Laana sat down. Simba Kongway went away, but soon returned with some game he had caught, and then he brought some fire, and the young man cooked the game and ate it. When he had finished he felt a great deal better, and they bade each other good-bye for the present, and each went his way.

After he had traveled another very long distance the youth came to a farm, and was met by a very, very old woman, who said to him: "Stranger, my husband has been taken very sick, and I am looking for some one to make him some medicine. Won't you make it?" But he answered: "My good woman, I am not a doctor, I am a hunter, and never used medicine in my life. I can not help you."

When he came to the road leading to the principal city he saw a well, with a bucket standing near it, and he said to himself: "That's just what I want. I'll take a drink of nice well-water. Let me see if the water can be reached."

As he peeped over the edge of the well, to see if the water was high enough, what should he behold but a great big snake, which, directly it saw him, said, "Son of Adam, wait a moment." Then it came out of the well and said: "How? Don't you know me?"

"I certainly do not," said the youth, stepping back a little.

"Well, well!" said the snake; "I could never forget you. I am Neeoka, whom you released from the trap. You know I said, 'Save me from the rain, and I will save you from the sun.' Now, you are a stranger in the town to which you are going; therefore hand me your little bag, and I will place in it the things that will be of use to you when you arrive there."

So 'Mvoo Laana gave Neeoka the little bag, and he filled it with chains of gold and silver, and told him to use them freely for his own benefit. Then they parted very cordially.

When the youth reached the city, the first man he met was he whom he had released from the trap, who invited him to go home with him, which he did, and the man's wife made him supper.

As soon as he could get away unobserved, the man went to the sultan and said: "There is a stranger come to my house with a bag full of chains of silver and gold, which he says he got from a snake that lives in a well. But although he pretends to be a man, I know that he is a snake who has the power to look like a man."

When the sultan heard this he sent some soldiers who brought 'Mvoo Laana and his little bag before him. When they opened the little bag, the man who was released from the trap persuaded the people that some evil would come out of it, and affect the children of the sultan and the children of the vizier.

Then the people became excited, and tied the hands of 'Mvoo Laana behind him.

But the great snake had come out of the well and arrived at the town just about this time, and he went and lay at the feet of the man who had said all those bad things about 'Mvoo Laana, and when the people saw this they said to that man: "How is this? There is the great snake that lives in the well, and he stays by you. Tell him to go away."

But Neeoka would not stir. So they untied the young man's hands, and tried in every way to make amends for having suspected him of being a wizard.

Then the sultan asked him, "Why should this man invite you to his home and then speak ill of you?"

And 'Mvoo Laana related all that had happened to him, and how the ape, the snake, and the lion had cautioned him about the results of doing any kindness for a man.

And the sultan said: "Although men are often ungrateful, they are not always so; only the bad ones. As for this fellow, he deserves to be put in a sack and drowned in the sea. He was treated kindly, and returned evil for good."

NDYAKUBI and NDALAKUBI

❖

Uganda (Baganda)

Once a man named Ndyakubi made blood-brotherhood with another man named Ndalakubi. Ndalakubi said to Ndyakubi, "Come and see me when you can." Ndyakubi agreed to do so, and after a time he went. Ndalakubi told his wife to cook a special meal for the visitor, which she did, and took the food to him, but it was not enough; he said he was still hungry when he had eaten what they supplied. Ndalakubi told his wife to cook a larger quantity of food, so she cooked as much as five men would eat and brought it to Ndyakubi, who ate it and still complained that he had not had enough. Ndalakubi told his wife to go to their friends and ask if they could help them, because all their food was finished. She went and brought back the food, cooked as much as would suffice a hundred men, and still Ndyakubi said he was not satisfied. Ndalakubi said, "I am sorry, but all my food is done." Ndyakubi said, "Very well, brother, I must go hungry, and die by the roadside from starvation."

Some time after this Ndalakubi went to see how Ndyakubi was. When he arrived Ndyakubi sent his wife to cook for the visitor, and she brought the food to Ndalakubi, who ate a little. Later on he asked where he was to sleep. Ndyakubi said, "I will let you have my bedstead." "But," said Ndalakubi, "there is no room for me to stretch myself." Ndyakubi took out a post from the house to make room for Ndalakubi. They then retired to rest, but Ndalakubi called out: "My friend, my feet are still outside," so Ndyakubi sent his wife to his friends and asked for reeds, and made an extension to the house, and they lay down again. Again

Ndalakubi called, "My friend, my feet are still outside; the wild animals will eat me." Nydakubi said, "What am I to do? All the reeds are done and I have no timber to build with."

Ndalakubi said, "When you came to visit me I had an immense amount of food cooked for you and you ate it all and still complained, and afterwards said: 'Let me go away and die in the road,' when I failed to satisfy you; what I say now is, Let the wild beasts come and eat me." Ndyakubi said, "No, my friend, curl yourself up and draw your legs inside and do not stretch yourself your full length, and when I come to your house I will eat a little and be satisfied. I am sorry for what I did." Ndalakubi said, "You did not say so before when I told you I was sorry the food ran short, you simply complained and grumbled. Now let me draw up my legs, and when you visit me again, eat properly and do not complain."

A TALE WHICH INCULCATES
KINDNESS to ANIMALS

Told by the old woman Nagatúu
Kenya (Kikuyu)

Once upon a time a young man married a girl named Ka-cham'-bi and brought her home, and the girl grew m'wé-li[1] in her shamba, and when the m'wéli was ripe she gathered it and brought it to her homestead; but a little bird called Kan-i-ó-ni-kan'-ga[2] came by and picked up grains of the m'wéli and ate it; and Kacham'bi picked up a stone and threw it at the bird, and said, "Go away, don't eat my grain." And this she did three times, and the third time she broke the leg of the bird. And the bird said, "Because you have broken my leg, harm will come to you." And he flew away.

After a while Kacham'bi became ill and bore a child, and the old woman who tended her went down to the stream to get water to wash the mother and the newborn infant. And when she got to the stream what should she see but the Kaniónikan'ga in the midst of the stream, spluttering with his wings and throwing water over him; and decked out like an M'kikúyu with necklaces of beads; and the old lady was so astonished at the sight that she stopped to look at him, and forgot all about the mother and the baby waiting in the hut; and another old woman came down to ask what had happened to her, and why she did not come back, and she, too, stood and gazed at the bird in his ornaments, and forgot to go back, and

---

1. Fine grain.
2. Described as a small bird—yellow breast—blue back—jumps along.

a third came, and a fourth, and then the rest of the people of the homestead all came down to the stream one by one till there was no one left in the village at all.

And at last Kacham'bi said, "I must go myself and see what is happening." So she got up, put down the babe into the bed, and left the hut; and when she came to the stream, what should she see but all the people gazing, and in the midst of the stream with all his ornaments, the Kaniónikan'ga whose leg she had broken. Now the bird, when he saw Kacham'bi, slipped out of the stream into the grass, and up to the hut, and found it empty, and he perched on the bed, and took the child's throat in his beak, and pinched it till the babe was suffocated, and when the mother came into the hut, there was the bird and her dead child. And the bird flew up to a tree, and all the people looked on, and he said, "I have done this to the woman because she would not give me grain and broke my leg; and I said I would work her ill, and so I have slain her child." Then Kacham'bi brought out corn and spread it on the ground plentifully, and the Kanionikan'ga ate and ate. And when he had eaten he flew back to the hut, and "made medicine," and perched again on the bed and the child breathed once more, and he said, "Because you have given me corn in plenty, I have given you back your child."

LOST AND FOUND

THE TALE of the MAIDEN WHO WAS SACRIFICED by HER KIN, and WHOM HER LOVER BROUGHT BACK from BELOW

Told by Na-ga-tú-u, mother of one of the herds of the Chief N'du-í-ni
Kenya (Kikuyu)

The sun was very hot and there was no rain, so the crops died, and hunger was great; and this happened one year, and again it happened a second, and yet a third year the rain failed; so the people all gathered together on the great open space on the hilltop, where they were wont to dance, and said each to the other, "Why does the rain delay in coming?" And they went to the Medicine-Man, and they said to him, "Tell us why there is no rain, for our crops have died, and we shall die of hunger?" And he took his gourd and poured out the lot, and this he did many times; and at last he said, "There is a maiden here who must be bought if rain is to fall, and the maiden is Wan-jí-ru. The day after tomorrow let all of you return to this place, and every one of you from the eldest to the youngest bring with him a goat for the purchase of the maiden."

So the day after the morrow, old men and young men all gathered together, and each brought in his hand a goat. Now they all stood in a circle, and the relations of Wanjíru stood together, and she herself stood in the middle; and as they stood the feet of Wanjíru began to sink into the ground; and she sank to her knees and cried aloud, "I am lost," and her father and mother also cried and said, "We are lost"; but those who looked on pressed close, and placed goats in the keeping of Wanjíru's father and mother. And Wanjíru went lower to her waist, and she cried aloud, "I am lost, but much rain will come"; and she sank to her breast: but the rain did not come, and she said again, "Much rain will come"; then she sank to her neck, and the rain came in great drops, and her people would have rushed forward to save her, but those who stood around pressed into their hands more goats, and they desisted.

So she said, "My people have undone me," and sank to her eyes, and as one after another of her family stepped forward to save her, one of the crowd would give to him or her a goat, and he fell back. And Wanjíru cried aloud for the last time, "I am undone, and my own people have done this thing." And she vanished from sight, and the earth closed over her, and the rain poured down, not, as you sometimes see it, in showers, but in a great deluge, and every one hastened to their own homes.

Now there was a young warrior who loved Wanjíru, and he lamented continually, saying, "Wanjíru is lost, and her own people have done this thing." And he said, "Where has Wanjíru gone? I will go to the same place." So he took his shield, and put in his sword and spear. And he wandered over the country day and night; and at last, as the dusk fell, he came to the spot where Wanjíru had vanished, and he stood where she had stood, and, as he stood, his feet began to sink as hers had sunk; and he sank lower and lower till the ground closed over him, and he went by a long road under the earth as Wanjíru had gone, and at length he saw the maiden. But, indeed, he pitied her sorely, for her state was miserable, and her raiment had perished. He said to her, "You were sacrificed to bring the rain; now the rain has come, I will take you back." So he took her on his back like a child, and brought her to the road he had traversed, and they rose together to the open air, and their feet stood once more on the ground, and he said, "You shall not return to the house of your people, for they have treated you shamefully." And he bade her wait till nightfall; and when it was dark he took her to the house of his mother, and he asked his mother to leave, and said he had business, and he allowed no one to enter. But his mother said, "Why do you hide this thing from me, seeing I am your mother who bore you?" So he suffered his mother, but he said, "Tell no one that Wanjíru is returned."

So she abode in the house of his mother; and then she and his mother slew goats, and Wanjíru ate the fat and grew strong; and of the skins they made garments for her, so that she was attired most beautifully.

It came to pass that the next day there was a great dance, and her lover went with the throng; but his mother and the girl waited till every one had assembled at the dance, and all the road was empty, and they came out of the house and mingled with the crowd; and the relations saw Wanjíru, and said, "Surely that is Wanjíru whom we had lost"; and they pressed to greet her, but her lover beat them off, for he said, "You sold Wanjíru shamefully." And she returned to his mother's house. But on the fourth day her family again came, and the warrior repented, for he said, "Surely they are her father and her mother and her brothers." So he paid them the purchase price, and he wedded Wanjíru who had been lost.

THE STORY of MPOBE

❂

Uganda (Baganda)

There was once a hunter named Mpobe, who was an expert in hunting the edible rat (musu). One day as he was sitting in his house, he saw a friend, Omuzizi, come running towards him, who said, "Come and let us hunt the rat." Mpobe agreed to go and took his hunting net and his dogs, and they went off together to the place where the game was known to abound. Omuzizi told Mpobe to stop at a certain place while he went on to fix the net to catch the animals; when he had fixed it he called to Mpobe to let the dogs loose; the latter then fastened the bells to one dog and turned them loose.

The dogs soon started a fine rat and went after it, but it turned and ran to one side where there was no one standing and no net to stop it. Mpobe said, "Never mind, the dogs will catch it," and he followed them, leaving his companions by the net. Omuzizi waited until sunset for Mpobe and then took the net and went home. The rat ran on and the dogs after it, and Mpobe after the dogs, until it entered a large hole, and the dogs dashed in after it; when Mpobe reached the hole he could hear the bells and followed the sound of them.

They went on until the rat came to a number of people: it rushed past them with the dogs close after it. When Mpobe came up, he was surprised to see the people, a large garden, and many houses. He asked the people if they had seen his dogs; they replied that they had, and pointed out the way they had gone. So he followed, though he was afraid, and at length he came upon his dogs with the rat standing near an important-looking person.

Mpobe fell down before him and greeted him, and Death (for it was he) asked him where he came from. Mpobe answered that he came "from above" where he had been hunting, and told him how he had followed his dogs into the hole and on until he reached that spot. Death then asked him what he had seen since he entered his country. Mpobe said he had not had time to look about him, because he was so busy following the dogs. Death then told him to return to his home, and warned him not to tell anyone where he had been, nor to mention what he had seen; he said, "You must not tell your father, mother, wife, nor any of your brothers"; Mpobe promised to obey, and said he would not speak about the place. Death threatened him that if ever he did so he would kill him.

Mpobe then returned home with his rat; his wife congratulated him upon his return, and went to cook his food. After the meal she asked her husband, "Have you been in the field all the time since you went away?" He replied, "Yes, I went to hunt the rat and stayed all night hunting it." His father came later on, and asked him where he had been hunting all the time. Mpobe replied, "I was in the field hunting all the time." After some days Mpobe's mother came to see him, and found him alone and asked him, "Were you really in the field all those days? What did you eat and drink?" Her son replied, "As I have said I was there, I am not going to tell you anything further, you can go and ask others and listen to what they say." She answered, "Mpobe, tell me just a little, please do." Mpobe answered, "I will tell you just a little, but do not tell anyone else." His mother promised she would not, so Mpobe told her how he followed his dogs, how he entered into the hole, and came to the land of the dead, where he saw numbers of people. He told her how fearful he was, how he asked the people to tell him the way the dogs had gone, how he had come upon Death and found his dogs and the rat, how he had been sent back with the rat, and how he thanked Death. He further told how Death had asked his name and warned him not to tell anyone his experiences on pain of death. His mother left him after hearing the story and returned home.

In the evening when it was dark Mpobe heard someone calling him, "Mpobe! Mpobe!" and he replied, "I am here. What do you want?" Death said, "What did I tell you?" Mpobe said, "You told me not to tell what I had seen at your place, and, Sir, I have only told my Mother a little." Death said, "I will leave you time to settle up your affairs, you must die when you have expended your property." Mpobe was silent, he had nothing to answer. Death therefore repeated his words, so Mpobe answered, "Let me sell all I have, and live upon the proceeds before I die." He sold first his child and bought a cow with the money and killed it, and ate it very slowly; a year passed, and indeed many years before he had come to an end of all his property.

Death called to him and asked if he had not consumed everything. Mpobe said he had not; he tried to hide away in the forest where Death would not find him, but Death said, "Mpobe! Why are you hiding in the forest? Do not think I cannot see you." He tried all kinds of different places wherein to hide, but Death always discovered him. At last he returned to his house and said, "Let me remain here and let Death come to me, because it is useless to try to hide from him." Death came and asked, "Mpobe, have you finished your wealth?" He replied, "I have finished it all," so Death took him. Hence comes the saying, "To be worried into telling a secret killed Mpobe." If he had not told his Mother, Death would not have killed him.

THE GIANT of
the GREAT WATER[1]

Told by an M'kikúyu employed as porter Kenya (Kikuyu)

There was once a small boy who was herding the goats, and his father came and pointed out to him some long and luxurious grass, and told him to take them there to feed. So he pastured them there that day, and took them there again the day following. Now the next day while the goats were feeding the owner of the pasture appeared, and he said to the boy, "Why are you feeding your goats on my grass?" And the boy said, "It is not my doing, for my father told me to come here." And he said, "This evening I will go to your father's house and talk to him." Now the owner of the grazing ground was a man very big and tall, and his name was Mukun'ga M'Búra, so in the evening he came to the home of the boy and he said to the father, "Why were your goats eating my grass when you could see I had closed it?"[2]

The father said, "That is my affair." So he said, "As you have done this, I will eat you and all your people," to which the father replied, "You shall do no such thing." So the young men made sharp their swords and got ready their spears, but Mukun'ga M'Búra was too strong for them, and he ate the father, and the young men, and the women, and the children, and the oxen, and the goats, and then he ate the house and the barns, so that there was nothing left. The only person who

---

1.   This story deals with the Rainbow (Mukun'ga M'Búra, literally "snake-rain") in its mythical aspect of a predatory monster which lives in water.
2.   *i.e.* had put up the usual signs to show that medicine had been made to protect it from trespassers.

escaped was the little boy, who ran away and hid in the grass so that Mukun'ga M'Búra did not see him.

Now he made himself a bow and shot wild game, and became very strong and built himself a house; and at last he said, when he was full grown, "Why do I stay here? I am big and strong. Mukun'ga M'Búra, who killed my father and all my people, still lives." So he took his sword and made it very sharp, and went to the district where Mukun'ga M'Búra lived, and as he drew near he saw him coming up out of the great water where he lived. He shouted to him, "To-morrow I will come and kill you." And he went back and ate more meat so as to be stronger than ever. The next day he went again, but Mukun'ga M'Búra was not to be seen; but the third day he met him again, and he said, "You have killed all my people, so I will kill you," and Mukun'ga M'Búra was afraid and said to the warrior, "Do not strike me with your sword over the heart or I shall die, but open my middle finger," so the warrior did so, and he said, "Make a big hole, not a little one." And the warrior made a big hole, and out came first the father, whom Mukun'ga M'Búra had eaten, and then the young men, and the women, and the cattle, and the sheep, and the houses, and the food stores just as before. And Mukun'ga M'Búra said, "You will not now kill me?" And the warrior said, "No, I will spare you for you have restored my father, his people and his goods, but you must not again eat them"; and he said, "They shall be safe."

The warrior and his people went back and rebuilt their homesteads, but the warrior thought to himself, "Now this Mukun'ga M'Búra is big and strong and very bad. He has eaten many people. He may come again and destroy my father."

So he called the young men and asked them to come and fight Mukun'ga M'Búra with him, and they all made ready for war and went to the home of Mukun'ga M'Búra. He saw them coming and said, "Why are you here to slay me? Have I not given you back your people?" But the warrior replied, "You are very evil; you have killed and eaten many people; therefore you shall die." Then they all fell upon him and slew him, and cut off his head and hewed his body in pieces. But a big piece separated itself from the rest of the body, which was dead, and went back into the water, and the warrior returned to his home and told his brothers that he had slain Mukun'ga M'Búra, all but one leg; "but to-morrow," he said,

"I will go into the water and get that leg and burn it." And the mother besought him not to go, but the next day he went, and when he got to the place there was no water to be seen, only cattle and goats, for what remained of Mukun'ga M'Búra had gathered together his children and taken all the water and gone very far, but the beasts he had not taken but left behind. So the warrior went back and brought his people, and they gathered the cattle and goats together, and took them back to their own homestead.

THE STORY of the LOST SISTER

🍂

Told by the old woman Nagatúu
Kenya (Kikuyu)

Once upon a time there were a brother and sister who lived together, and the mother died leaving many goats, and the brother looked after the goats in the daytime, but in the evening he went away from home, for he was very beautiful, and had many friends. The name of the girl was Wa-ché-ra, the name of the brother Wa-m'wé-a.

Now one day when the brother returned Wachéra said to him, "Two men were here yesterday, and if you go away and leave me they will carry me off," but he said, "You talk nonsense," and she said, "I am speaking the truth, but when they take me I will bear with me a gourd full of sap which is like fat, and along the path I will let it drop, so that you can follow my trail."[1] Now that night when Wam'wéa brought the goats home, Wachéra made a great feast and gruel, but again he went away. And when Wam'wéa came back next morning he found the homestead empty, for his sister had been carried away as she said, but he saw the track where drop by drop she had let fall the sap which is like fat. And Wam'wéa followed over hill and down dale, and ever and again he heard her voice crying from the opposite hill side, "Follow after where you see the trail." The following day the sap began to take root, and to spring up into little plants, but his sister he saw not. And at last he returned to his home to herd the flock, and he took them out to feed, but he had no one to prepare food for him when he returned at night, and if he himself

---

1.   The wild gourd when ripe contains a soft pulp in which are its seeds. This pulp resembles the liquid fat obtained by melting the sheep's tail.

prepared the food there was no one to care for the flocks, so he slew a goat and ate it, and when it was finished he slew yet another, and so on till all the goats were finished. Then he killed and ate the oxen one by one, and they lasted him months and years for the flock was large, but at last they were all gone, and then he bethought him of his sister.

Now the plants which had sprung were by this time grown to trees, which marked the way she had gone, and so he journeyed on for one month and half a month, and at the end of that time he came to a stream, and by the stream were two children getting water, and he said to the younger, "Give me some water in your gourd," but the child refused; but the elder child spoke to the younger and said, "Give the stranger to drink, for our mother said if ever you see a stranger coming by the way of the trees he is my brother." So he and the children went up to the homestead, and he waited outside, and Wachéra came out, and he knew her at once, but she did not know him, for he was not dressed as before with ochre and fat; and he came into her hut, and she gave him food, not in a good vessel, but in a potsherd, and he slept in the hut, but on the floor, not on the bed.

Now next day he went out with the children to drive away the birds from the crops, and as he threw a stone he would say, "Fly away, little bird, as Wachéra flew away and never came back any more," and another bird would come, and he would throw another stone and say the same words again, and this happened the next day and the next for a whole month; and the children heard, and so did others, and said, "Why does he say the name Wachéra?" And they went and told their mother, and at last she came and waited among the grass and listened to his words, and said, "Surely this is my brother Wam'wéa," and she went back to the house and sent for a young man, and told him to go and fetch Wam'wéa to come to her, for she said, "He is my brother." And the young man went and told Wam'wéa the words of his sister, but he refused, for he said, "I have dwelt in the abode of my sister, and she has given me no cup for my food but a potsherd," and he would not go in. And the young man returned to Wachéra, and told her the words of her brother, and she said, "Take ten goats and go again and bid him come to me," and the young man took ten goats and said, "Thy sister has sent these ten goats," but Wam'wéa refused, and the young man returned. And Wachéra said, "Take ten oxen and give them to my brother," but Wam'wéa would not; and Wachéra sent him ten cows, and again ten cows, and still Wam'wéa refused to come in. And Wachéra told her husband how she had found her brother, and how he would not be reconciled to her, and her husband said, "Send him yet more beasts," so Wachéra sent ten other cows and again ten more, till Wam'wéa had received forty cows besides the goats and the oxen which Wachéra had sent at the first, and the heart of Wam'wéa relented, and he came into the house of his sister. And she killed a goat, and took the fat and dressed his hair and his shoulders, for she said, "I did not know you, for you were not adorned as before."

After Wam'wéa had been reconciled to his sister, he decided that eight wives should be given him, so the husband of Wachéra sent to all his relations round about, and they brought in goats, and Wam'wéa bought eight girls, some for thirty goats, some for forty. Other relations all came and built eight huts for the wives near to the dwelling of Wachéra, so Wam'wéa and his wives dwelt near the homestead of his sister.

LEGEND REGARDING ORIGIN of FIRE[1]

Kenya (Kikuyu)

A long time ago a man borrowed a spear, *katimu*, from a neighbour to kill a porcupine which was destroying his crops. He lay in wait in the field and eventually speared one, but it was only wounded and ran off with the spear in its body and disappeared down a burrow. He went to the owner and told him that the spear was lost, but the owner insisted on having it back. Whereupon, the man bought a new spear and offered it to the owner in place of the lost weapon, but the owner refused it and again insisted on the return of the original spear. The man then proceeded to crawl down the porcupine burrow, and having crawled a long way found himself eventually, to his surprise, in a place where many people were sitting about cooking food by a fire. They asked him what he wanted and he told them of his errand. They then invited him to stay and eat with them; he was afraid and said he could not stay as he must go back with the spear which he saw lying there. They made no effort to keep him, but told him to climb up the roots of a *mugumu* tree, which penetrated down into the cavern, and said that he would soon come out into the upper world. They gave him some fire to take back with him. So he took the spear and the fire and climbed out as he was told.

This is said to be the way fire came to man; before that people ate their food raw.

When the man reached his friends he returned the spear and said to the owner, "You have caused me a great deal of trouble to recover your spear, and if you want

---

1.   The underworld referred to in this tale is called *Miri ya mikeongoi.*

some of this fire which you see going away into smoke, you will have to climb up the smoke and get it back for me." The owner of the spear tried and tried to climb the smoke but could not do it, and the elders then came and intervened and said, "We will make the following arrangement: fire shall be for the use of all, and because you have brought it you shall be our chief."

THE GIRL and the DOVES

Told by the old woman Nagatúu
Kenya (Kikuyu)

Long ago a girl child called Wan-jí-ru was beaten by her mother so severely that her back was broken and she died, and the doves—(du-tú-ra)—came and gathered up her bones amongst the grass, and joined them together by means of little chains like women wear, and one who was very clever joined her back together. And she became alive again, and they found a house for her in a cave by the riverside.

Now three children came down to the opposite bank of the river to get water, and one was the younger sister of Wanjíru; and when the gourds were filled they each helped the other up with them onto their backs to carry home. But when it came to the turn of Wanjíru's sister, they refused, for they said, "Your mother beat your sister and killed her, so we will not help you," and they went away, and the little girl sat down and cried; and as she cried, Wanjíru came out of her home among the stones and came across the water, and took the gourd and helped her to put it on her back. But she said, "Do not tell any one at home that you have seen me"—and this same thing happened many days. At last her mother noticed that the child always came home after the others, and she said, "Who helps you to lift up your gourd? Surely you are always last?" And she said, "I went among the grass, and there slipt it up myself." But her mother persisted, and at last the child told, and said, "I have seen my sister Wanjíru, who was dead, and she has helped me."

So the next day when the children went down for water, the father and mother went too, and hid among the grass, and waited, and when Wanjíru came, as was her custom, to help with the gourd, they sprang up and seized her and took her home.

Then the doves all gathered together and flew to the home of Wanjíru, and they said to the mother, "Give us the chains you wear as ornaments," and the mother refused. So then they took back the chains they had given to make Wanjíru, and the one who was an expert took out from her head the long chain he had put in to join up the bones of her back, and all her bones fell to pieces again as before, and the doves flew away. Then the mother took all the bones and put them in the cave where Wanjíru had lived.

And the doves came once more and put Wanjíru together again, but they said, "You must not help your sister when she comes for water." But when she thought the doves were not looking, and the child came, Wanjíru helped her as before; but the doves saw her and said again, "You must not help your sister, or we will again undo our work and you will die." So Wanjíru refrained.

A NOTE ON THE SOURCES

✦

The stories in this collection were recorded and translated by professional and amateur folklorists and anthropologists in the early 20th century. They represent only a sampling of East African folklore. There is no one definition of which regions and cultures constitute East Africa, so by necessity, this collection is not comprehensive. However, readers who enjoy these tales are encouraged to seek out further stories from this rich tradition.

In cases where the original source provided the information, we have included the name or identification of the original storyteller. The same applies to the geographical information accompanying each story; we have included not only the country that now encompasses the region where the story was first recorded, but also the name of the tribe or culture to which the storyteller belonged, whenever possible.

The stories have been excerpted from the following publications, all of which are in the public domain:

Bateman, George W. *Zanzibar Tales*. Reprint of the A. C. McClure & Co. 1901 Chicago edition, Internet Archive, 2007. https://archive.org/details/zanzibartalestol00batcuoft

Hobley, C. W. *Bantu Beliefs and Magic*. Reprint of the H. F. & G. Witherby 1922 London edition, Internet Archive, 2017. https://archive.org/details/bantubeliefsmagi00hobl/page/n287

———. *Ethnology of the A-Kamba and Other East African Tribes*. Reprint of the Cambridge University Press 1910 London edition, Internet Archive, 2007. https://archive.org/details/ethnologyofakamb00hobluoft/page/iv

Roscoe, Rev. John. *The Baganda: An Account of Their Native Customs and Beliefs*. Reprint of the Macmillan and Co. 1911 London edition, Internet Archive, 2008. https://archive.org/details/bagandaaccountof00roscuoft

Routledge, Katherine and W. Scoresby Routledge. *With a Prehistoric People: The Akikúyu of British East Africa*. Reprint of the Edward Arnold 1910 London edition, Internet Archive, 2009. https://archive.org/details/withprehistoricp00rout

SOURCES

The Ape, the Snake, and the Lion
From *Zanzibar Tales*

The Cat and the Fowl
From *The Baganda: an account of their native customs and beliefs*

The Giant of the Great Water
From *With a Prehistoric People, the Akikuyu of British East Africa*

The Girl and the Doves
From With a Prehistoric People, the Akikuyu of British East Africa

Haamdaanee
From *Zanzibar Tales*

The Hare and the Lion
From *Zanzibar Tales*

Kiwobe and His Sheep
From *The Baganda: an account of their native customs and beliefs*

Legend Regarding Origin of Fire
From Bantu Beliefs and Magic

The Magician and the Sultan's Son
From *Zanzibar Tales*

Mkaaah Jeechonee, the Boy Hunter
From *Zanzibar Tales*

The Monkey, the Shark, and the Washerman's Donkey
From *Zanzibar Tales*

Ndyakubi and Ndalakubi
From *The Baganda: an account of their native customs and beliefs*

Sifirwakange and Kasokambirye
From *The Baganda: an account of their native customs and beliefs*

The Story of Mpobe
From *The Baganda: an account of their native customs and beliefs*

The Story of M'Wambía and the N'Jengé
From *With a Prehistoric People, the Akikuyu of British East Africa*

The Story of the Girl Who Cut the Hair of the N'Jengé
From *With a Prehistoric People, the Akikuyu of British East Africa*

The Story of the Hare, Ki-Kamba-Wa-paruku or Buku
From *Ethnology of A-Kamba*

The Story of the Lost Sister
From *With a Prehistoric People, the Akikuyu of British East Africa*

The Story of the Ngu or Tortoise and the Kipalala or Fish Eagle
From *Ethnology of A-Kamba*

The Tale of the Maiden Who Was Sacrificed by Her Kin, and Whom Her Lover Brought Back from Below
From *With a Prehistoric People, the Akikuyu of British East Africa*

A Tale Which Inculcates Kindness to Animals
From *With a Prehistoric People, the Akikuyu of British East Africa*

Wokubira Omulalu mu Kyama
From *The Baganda: an account of their native customs and beliefs*